He Collapsed Against Her, Sandwiching Her Body Between The Scorching Heat Of His And The Hardness Of The Staircase.

Floating on a haze of satiation, she pressed her lips to his throat and tasted the salty tang of his skin.

She laid a hand over Sawyer's pounding heart and struggled for comprehension. What had just happened? And why now with Sawyer? Every cell in her body pulsed with life. Her heart thundered, and the numbness she'd known for years had vanished. Her late husband's lovemaking—if you could call it that—had never moved her the way his brother's desperate coupling had. Even in the midst of madness, Sawyer had ensured her pleasure, but even before her body cooled, regrets forced themselves forward.

Dear heavens, what had she done?

Dear Reader,

Welcome to another stellar month of smart, sensual reads. Our bestselling series DYNASTIES: THE DANFORTHS comes to a compelling conclusion with Leanne Banks's *Shocking the Senator* as honest Abe Danforth finally gets his story. Be sure to look for the start of our next family dynasty story when Eileen Wilks launches DYNASTIES: THE ASHTONS next month and brings you all the romance and intrigue you could ever desire…all set in the fabulous Napa Valley.

Award-winning author Jennifer Greene is back this month to conclude THE SCENT OF LAVENDER series with the astounding *Wild in the Moment*. And just as the year brings some things to a close, new excitement blossoms as Alexandra Sellers gives us the next installment of her SONS OF THE DESERT series with *The Ice Maiden's Sheikh*. The always-enjoyable Emilie Rose will wow you with her tale of *Forbidden Passion*—let's just say the book starts with a sexy tryst on a staircase. We'll let you imagine the rest. Brenda Jackson is also back this month with her unforgettable hero Storm Westmoreland, in *Riding the Storm*. (A title that should make you go hmmm.) And rounding things out is up-and-coming author Michelle Celmer's second book, *The Seduction Request*.

I would love to hear what you think about Silhouette Desire, so please feel free to drop me a line c/o Silhouette Books, 233 Broadway, Suite 1001, New York, NY 10279. Let me know what miniseries you are enjoying, your favorite authors and things you would like to see in the future.

With thanks,

Melissa Jeglinski

Melissa Jeglinski
Senior Editor
Silhouette Desire

Forbidden Passion

EMILIE ROSE

Silhouette®
Desire

Published by Silhouette Books
America's Publisher of Contemporary Romance

Virginia and Angie, thanks for
your help and your patience.

SILHOUETTE BOOKS

ISBN 0-373-76624-6

FORBIDDEN PASSION

This edition published by arrangement with Harlequin Books S.A.

Visit Silhouette Books at www.eHarlequin.com

Printed in U.S.A.

Books by Emilie Rose

Silhouette Desire

Expecting Brand's Baby #1463
The Cowboy's Baby Bargain #1511
The Cowboy's Million-Dollar Secret #1542
A Passionate Proposal #1578
Forbidden Passion #1624

EMILIE ROSE

lives in North Carolina with her college sweetheart husband and four sons. This bestselling author's love for romance novels developed when she was twelve years old and her mother hid them under sofa cushions each time Emilie entered the room. Emilie grew up riding and showing horses. She's a devoted baseball mom during the season and can usually be found in the bleachers watching one of her sons play. Her hobbies include quilting, cooking (especially cheesecake) and anything cowboy. Her favorite TV shows include Discovery Channel's medical programs, *ER, CSI* and *Boston Public.* Emilie's a country music fan because there's an entire book in nearly every song.

Emilie loves to hear from her readers and can be reached at P.O. Box 20145, Raleigh, NC 27619 or at www.EmilieRose.com.

One

Her husband. She'd loved him. She'd hated him. And now he was gone. Guilt and pain seeped through Lynn Riggan, chilling her to the bone. She'd wanted to end her marriage, but not this way. Never this way.

Eager to shed her painful four-inch heels and a dress so tight she hadn't been able to sit down all day, she closed the front door behind the last of the mourners and sagged against it. God, she hated this dress, but it was the only black one she owned that wasn't cut to reveal more cleavage than she felt comfortable displaying at a funeral, and Brett had liked it. She took comfort in the fact that today was the last time she'd have to dress to impress someone else.

"Are you all right?" Her brother-in-law's quiet baritone scraped over her raw nerves.

She clenched her teeth, swallowed hard and opened her eyes. Straightening, she folded her hands at her waist and forced a smile she did not feel. Her lips quivered, and she knew she hadn't fooled Sawyer when his dark brows dipped with concern.

He crossed the cool marble foyer and stopped in front of her. "Lynn?"

"I thought you'd left." She wished he had because she hated for him to see her this way. Weak. Needy. Her world was falling apart, and she didn't have the strength to pretend everything would be all right—not even for Sawyer's sake.

"I stepped out back for a minute." Losing his beloved baby brother had been hard on him. Grief filled his cobalt-blue eyes and deepened the laugh lines fanning from the corners. A muscle ticked in the tense line of his chiseled jaw. His ruggedly handsome features were drawn and pale, and his shiny dark hair looked as if the late-spring breeze or restless fingers had tumbled it. The rigid set of his broad shoulders beneath his black suit revealed how tightly he held his emotions in check.

"You should go home and rest, Sawyer." Please leave before I crumble.

"Yeah. Probably. But I feel so damned…empty." He shoved a hand through his inky hair, mussing it even more. A lock curled over his forehead, making him look more like a college boy than the thirty-two-year-old CEO of a privately owned computer software company. "I keep waiting for Brett to come through that door laughing and shouting, *'Gotcha.'*"

Yes, Brett had liked cruel jokes. She'd been the butt of several. His worst joke yet was the financial mess he'd left for her to unravel. But even he couldn't have faked the fiery car accident that had taken his life.

Sawyer's eyes lasered in on hers. "Will you be all right here alone?"

Alone. Already the walls of this mausoleum of a house closed in on her. Right now she needed a hug more than anything, but she'd learned how to survive without that simple comfort a long time ago. She chewed her lip, wrapped her arms around her middle and avoided his probing gaze. "I'll be fine."

Her eyes burned from lack of sleep, and her muscles ached from pacing the floor all night. She wished she'd never found that key in the plastic bag of personal effects the hospital personnel had given her. If she hadn't found the key, she wouldn't have opened the safe. And if she hadn't opened the safe... She took one shaky breath and then another trying to ward off panic.

What was she going to do?

She'd been searching for a life insurance policy to cover the funeral costs, and instead she'd discovered statements from empty bank accounts and a private journal in which her husband had written that he'd never loved her, that he found her such a dud in bed that he'd turned to another woman for pleasure. He'd catalogued her faults in excruciating detail.

"Lynn?" Sawyer lifted her chin with the warm tip of his finger. "Do you want me to stay tonight? I could bunk in the guest room."

No, he couldn't. She'd moved to the guest room months ago, and if he saw her personal belongings in the room he'd know that all wasn't right in the Riggan household. She didn't want to tell Sawyer that she and Brett had been having trouble for months, and she'd suspected her husband might be having an affair. She'd even consulted a lawyer about a divorce, but Brett had blamed their problems on his workload and charmed her into giving him one more chance. Against her better judgment, she'd allowed him to convince her that a baby would bring them closer, and they'd slept together one last time—just moments before she'd found proof of his infidelity, lost her temper and kicked him out of the house. Minutes later he'd died in the car crash.

"No, I'm okay." Her voice cracked over the last word and a tremor worked through her. She had no money, no job, and no way to pay for this extravagant house Brett had insisted they buy. The house and car payments were due, and she had no idea how she'd make them. As if that weren't enough…

Her nerves stretched to the breaking point. She pressed a hand to her belly and prayed that the intimacy with her husband three nights ago wouldn't result in a child. She loved children, and she'd always wanted a large family, but she didn't know how she'd take care of herself right now, let alone a baby.

Sawyer pulled her into his arms, breaking her train of self-pity. After a stiff moment, she laid her head on his shoulder and selfishly allowed herself to savor the comforting warmth of the strong arms enfolding her and the softness of his suit against her cheek. A sob hiccuped past the knot in her throat. She mashed her lips together, clenched her teeth and stiffened her spine. She was not a quitter. She would survive this.

"Shhh," he murmured against her temple. The whisper of his breath swept her skin, and his hands chafed her spine. The spicy scent of his cologne invaded her senses. A shiver of another kind worked over her. Appalled, she tried to pull free, but his arms held fast. His chest shuddered against hers, and a warm, wet trail burned down her neck. Sawyer's tears.

Her throat clogged and her heart squeezed in sympathy. Sawyer had stood beside her through identifying Brett's body and every step of the funeral arrangements.

The fact that he'd hidden his grief and been strong for her up to this point made his loss of control more heart-wrenching. She focused on his pain rather than her own. It was safer that way, because hers was tied up with so many other emotions. Disappointment. Failure. Anger. Betrayal. Guilt.

"It'll be okay." She parroted the meaningless words she'd heard a dozen times in the past three days. "We'll get through this, Sawyer, one day at a time."

Wanting to offer him the comfort she sorely needed herself, she wrapped her arms around his middle, held him close and patted his back. She whispered soothing nonsense into his ear, but nothing she could say or do would change the past. She couldn't bring Brett back.

Sawyer's arms tightened around her and his chest pressed against her breasts in a warm, solid wall. He lowered his head and tucked his face into the side of her neck. His breath heated her skin. A spark flared in her midsection. She tried to ignore it, but it had been years since she'd been held tenderly, and she'd been frozen inside for so long by her husband's callous treatment. It wasn't Sawyer's fault that her needy body misinterpreted his consoling gesture.

His breath shuddered in and out as if he struggled for control. He loosened his arms, straightened and drew back an inch. Swiping a hand over his face, he grimaced. "I'm sorry. I just needed a minute."

"It's okay." Seeing this strong man break nearly undid her. She rose on her tiptoes to kiss his cheek, but he turned his head unexpectedly. Their cheeks and noses brushed and her pulse skittered. Drawing a sharp breath, she eased back on her heels. The lapels of his suit coat scraped across the thin fabric of her snug dress, and the resulting tingle in her breasts and belly alarmed her. Shamed her. How could her body respond to Sawyer's, but not to her own husband's?

Brett's last damning words, *Frigid bitch,* echoed in her ears. She hadn't been frigid until he'd hurt her, selfishly taking what he wanted without concern for her pleasure. After that something had curled up inside her each time he'd touched her. She'd dreaded the intimate side of their marriage because it represented her failure as wife and a woman.

"I want to forget." Sawyer's anguished whisper shredded her heart and weakened the emotional dam she'd built around her fragile emotions.

"I know. Me, too." She traced the deep groove grief had etched in his cheek with an unsteady hand. His afternoon beard stubble abraded her fingertips. The raspy sensation traveled up her arm like a mild electric current. She yanked her hand away and wiped her tingling palm against her hip.

Scant inches separated their lips, and their breaths mingled. The pain in Sawyer's eyes slowly changed into surprise and then into something else—something that warmed her, scared her, made her heart race and her muscles tense, but she couldn't look away. She wet her lips and searched in vain for the words to end this awkward, forbidden moment.

Sawyer's dark lashes swept down to conceal his expression. Before she could step back, his hands cupped her elbows and his mouth crushed hers in a desperate kiss. Shock held her rigid, but what stunned her more than the unexpected kiss was her reaction to it. A heady rush of desire transported her back to the night of her last date with Sawyer when she'd thought he might be "the one." Back to the time before her heart had been broken and Brett had come into her life, when she'd felt beautiful and desirable instead of ugly and unresponsive, and she'd still held hope for her future instead of despair.

Sawyer withdrew and their gazes locked for one paralyzing moment. He lifted an unsteady hand to gently stroke her face and cup her jaw in the warmth of his palm. His thumb skated over her damp bottom lip and her breath hitched. Moving slowly, as if giving her the option to object, he bent over her again, peppering kisses over her forehead and cheeks.

Stop this insanity, she thought. But her body had been numb for so long, and Sawyer's touch awakened her as if he'd pushed the stone away from the entrance to the cave where her soul had been entombed for the past four years. Heat seeped through her, thawing the parts of her that her husband had numbed with his caustic comments.

Sawyer's lips touched hers again, this time gentling and clinging before withdrawing a scant inch. His breath hissed in and out, once, twice, sweeping over her skin like a dense seductive fog, before he took her mouth hungrily.

Lynn's blood swept through her veins like a hot desert wind, warming her, stirring her, and her lips parted in a stunned gasp. His tongue found hers. During her marriage she'd become accustomed to Brett's gagging, conquering kisses, but she had no clue how to handle Sawyer's gentle persuasion. Her skin grew damp and tingly instead of crawling with revulsion. She tentatively touched her tongue to the slick heat of his, and his grip on her arms tightened, though his embrace wasn't painful. She wouldn't bear bruises once this lunacy ended. And it should end. *Now.* But she didn't have the will or the strength to break away.

His hands skimmed gently over the sides of her breasts and the curve of her waist before settling on her hips. Her senses rioted and her head spun.

"Tell me to stop," he whispered against her lips, but even though his words urged her away, the hands splaying over her bottom pulled her closer.

The heat of his body permeated the fabric of her dress from her knees to her shoulders. His hard planes fused to her soft curves, and the thick ridge of his arousal pressed against her belly, shocking her. *Arousing* her. She couldn't have pushed him away if her life depended on it, and without his supporting arms, her weak knees would have folded. Curling her fingers into the lapels of his jacket, she held fast and tipped her head back to gasp for air.

She barely had time to draw a breath before Sawyer devoured her mouth with an unleashed hunger that should have frightened her. Instead it made her yearn for more. His hands kindled a fire within her, stroking her waist and then the sensitive skin beneath her breasts. A moan bubbled in her throat when he gently cupped her flesh and teased her taut nipples with his thumbs. His thigh nudged hers apart as much as her snug dress would allow, and hard, hot muscle pressed against her core.

Her belly ached with need—a need she hadn't felt in years. Her knees shook. What was she doing? Was she crazy? She couldn't bring herself to answer the questions. Brushing aside his jacket, she flattened her hands over the thin cotton of his shirt. His heart pounded against her palm, and hers raced just as fast.

He shrugged out of his suit coat with abrupt, jerky movements, tossed it aside and reached for her again. His cobalt gaze locked with hers. She couldn't look away. The fiery passion in his eyes made her tremble. Inside. Outside. All over.

His fingers tunneled through her upswept hair, sending pins pinging onto the marble floor seconds before the long, cool strands of her hair tumbled against her neck and shoulders. Sawyer took one audible breath and then another.

"Lynn." His rough voice pleaded, but for what she didn't know, and it didn't matter because her voice—along with her sanity, evidently—had left her. She couldn't think beyond the fact that Sawyer wanted her.

She touched a finger to the muscle ticking in his jaw. He angled his head, pressing his lips to her wrist, and then his lips parted and his tongue swirled an intoxicating pattern over her skin. Liquid fire surged through her.

His hands skated over her hips and then tunneled beneath the hem of her dress. Her breath lodged in her throat. His fingers burned against the back of her thighs and then through the thin silk of her panties. He kneaded her bottom once, twice. Cool air swept her thighs and then her buttocks as he hiked up her skirt and eased her panties down. His hot, long-fingered hands cupped and caressed bare skin with a gentleness that made her melt. Her entire body flushed and her head fell back. A hollow ache formed in her belly and a moan rose from her chest.

Sawyer nibbled her neck, her jaw, her earlobe. He nudged her backward until the first stair riser pressed her heels. When he urged her to sit she let her weak knees fold. The roughness of carpeted stair runner abraded her tender skin. Sawyer whisked her panties over her ankles, knelt between her knees and reached for his belt buckle. Her insides combusted and her heart jumped to her throat. She dug her nails into the carpet and struggled for sanity.

A fragment of her mind acknowledged what was going to happen if she didn't put an end to this madness. She *should* stop him, but her body tingled with awareness, and her pulse and the juncture of her thighs throbbed with life for the first time in years. She felt like a woman instead of a block of wood. She remained mute.

Rather than shove Sawyer away, she reached for him, helping him push his trousers over his lean hips, and then she burrowed her fingers beneath the hem of his shirt and clasped the supple skin at his waist. His body heat scorched her palms. Her pulse raced faster, and she gulped one lungful of air after another.

His breath whistled through clenched teeth, and his hands tightened on her thighs, easing them farther apart. He urged her back against the carpeted stairs and consumed her mouth with hot, intoxicating, sanity-robbing thoroughness. The thick head of his erection parted her folds, finding her wetness, and then he thrust deep. Air gushed from her lungs at the feeling of fullness.

It didn't hurt, a surprised voice echoed in her head before the brush of his thumb at the juncture of their bodies chased all rational thought from her mind. He thrust deep and stroked her, suckled her neck and caressed her bottom, pushing and chasing her on an uphill climb until she reached the top and tumbled over in a freefall of unfamiliar sensation.

Surprised, she dug her nails into the firm muscles of his buttocks as her body clenched around his in involuntary spasms. His teeth scraped against her collarbone, and then he groaned her name against her pounding pulse point.

Sawyer lunged and withdrew again and again. Twining her arms around him, Lynn held him tight and let the tide of sensation sweep her away. Her loosened muscles gave way and her thighs spread wider, allowing Sawyer to rock deeper inside her—deep enough to reach the portions of her soul that she'd hidden away. Cradling her face in his hands, he slammed his lips against hers, devouring her mouth and tangling tongues like a starving man. A responding hunger rekindled within her. He shifted the angle of his hips, creating a new friction against the sensitive flesh he'd plied so skillfully, and Lynn found herself climbing again. She arched to meet his thrusts. Sawyer shuddered and shivered, pulsing deep inside her core, and she tumbled over the precipice again.

He collapsed against her, sandwiching her body between the scorching heat of his and the hardness of the staircase. Their labored breaths echoed in the two-story foyer. Floating on a haze of satiation, she pressed her lips to his throat and tasted the salty tang of his skin. His chest hair tickled her lips, tantalized her cheek.

She laid a hand over Sawyer's pounding heart and struggled for comprehension. What had just happened? And why now with Sawyer? Every cell in her body pulsed with life. Her heart thundered, and the numbness she'd known for years had vanished. Brett's lovemaking—if you could call it that—had never moved her the way Sawyer's desperate coupling had. Even in the midst of madness, Sawyer had ensured her pleasure, but even before her body cooled, regrets forced themselves forward.

Dear heavens, what had she done?

* * *

Sweat dampened Sawyer's skin, adhering his shirt to his back. His heart hammered and he panted for breath.

Lynn shoved at his chest. The combination of panic and regret in her sky-blue eyes knotted his stomach, and then she looked at her wedding band, tightly closed her eyes and tucked her softly rounded chin to her chest.

What had he done? Regret hit him like a dagger in the heart. How could he have taken advantage of his brother's grieving widow? Stone-cold sober, he staggered to his feet, but his legs quivered beneath him as unsteady as a newborn colt's. Ashamed of his loss of control, he yanked up his pants and shoved in his shirttails. In his haste he nearly maimed himself with his zipper. He swore, and she flinched, biting her plump bottom lip until he expected to see blood. Her posture grew tenser by the second.

"I'm sorry, Lynn. That shouldn't have happened." He sounded as if he'd swallowed a bucket of rocks, but it was a miracle he got any words past the knot in his throat.

Looking everywhere but at him, she struggled to her feet and batted the hem of her dress over her long legs. She finger combed the tangles from her mussed golden hair with trembling hands.

He fisted his hands on the urge to help tame her silky tresses, and followed her horrified gaze to the black panties on the white marble floor by the front door. Self-disgust crawled over his skin. He'd lost control, yanked her skirt above her waist and taken her like some damned frat boy. Hell, they were both fully dressed except for her panties.

Ass. Idiot. What were you thinking?

"It's okay, Sawyer. We were both hurting and

wanted—*needed*—to forget for a moment. It won't happen again." The tightness of her voice and the pallor of her creamy skin belied her casual words.

"You want to forget what just happened?" Impossible. How could he forget the silkiness of her skin beneath his palms, the sweet taste of her mouth or the satiny, wet folds that had surrounded him?

"Yes, please." Her whispered plea destroyed him.

"Unless you're on the pill, forgetting might not be an option. I didn't use protection. I'm sorry. If it's any consolation, I've never been careless before."

She closed her eyes and swallowed visibly. Her thin black dress molded every tantalizing curve of her body, making the rise and fall of her breasts on shaky breaths hard to miss.

Get with the program, Riggan. She's your brother's wife. "Lynn, are you taking contraceptives?"

She mashed the bow of her lips into a flat line. Her chin quivered. "I'm tired. Would you excuse me?"

His gut knotted, and sweat beaded on his upper lip. "Lynn?"

Her finely arched brows dipped, and her eyes clouded. "I can't tell you what you want to hear. I'm not taking contraceptives and the timing…the timing isn't the best."

Hell. He caught her by her upper arms. "What are you saying? You could get pregnant now? How can you be sure?"

Every vestige of color faded from her delicate features, accentuating the dark circles under her eyes. A fine tremor worked its way through her body. The urge to pull her closer made him tighten his fingers before common sense rallied. Comforting her, taking comfort in her, had already gotten him into a world of trouble.

He'd crossed the line. Releasing her, he shoved his fists into his pockets and stepped back.

She lifted a trembling hand to cover the pulse leaping at the base of her throat. Her other hand spread over her flat belly, where even now their cells could be merging to create a new life. He couldn't even begin to put a name to the emotions the knowledge stirred inside him, and fighting the need to lay his hand over hers took everything he had.

"Brett and I were trying to start a family and we…" She ducked her chin. A rush of pink swept her high cheekbones before the curtain of her hair swept forward to conceal her features. "The day he died was the beginning of my fertile cycle."

His belly bottomed out. Could this day get any worse? He'd buried his baby brother, made love to his brother's wife and may have impregnated a woman he should be protecting, not hurting. And then her words sank in. She and Brett had been trying to make a baby. Brett had been the only family he had left, and his brother's seed might already be growing inside Lynn's womb. Sawyer clutched the link to Brett like a lifeline.

He might be an uncle.

Or a father. He swallowed the lump in his throat and struggled to breathe despite the constriction of his chest muscles. The first would be a blessing, the second a curse on his soul for taking what wasn't his and yet, *he liked the idea of Lynn having his baby.* The possibility tied his insides into knots—knots he couldn't unravel when his thoughts were as convoluted as this. He shoved the issue aside to deal with later, when he'd recovered a shred of reason.

He should leave, get the hell out of here before he made things worse, but he couldn't until he knew Brett had provided for Lynn. "I stayed behind because I need to know if Brett's life insurance will be enough to support you—" he swallowed again, but the tightness in his throat persisted "—and a child."

The silence stretched so long that he didn't think she'd answer, and then her gaze met his. She looked so damned fragile. He sucked a sharp breath at the worry in her eyes and battled the urge to pull her close.

"Brett let the policy lapse."

Great. His brother had never been one for what he considered trivial details. "What will you do?"

She shifted on her feet, reminding him that she was bare *and wet* beneath the skirt of her dress. Hell. He yanked his thoughts back on track.

Her jaw set. "I'd rather not discuss this now, Sawyer."

He fisted his hands in frustration. "I'm not trying to be callous. I know you're tired and it's been a rough day, and I've added to that, but I won't leave until I know you have enough money to cover immediate expenses."

"That's not your problem. If I have to I'll get a job."

"Doing what?"

"I don't know. I can always go back to waitressing."

Lynn had been a waitress in a downtown Chapel Hill coffee shop when he'd met her four and a half years ago. She'd lured him with her sunny smile, sky-blue eyes and sun-streaked blond hair, and then she'd hooked him with her contradictions. Her work uniform had consisted of a starched white shirt, pure schoolmarm, and a short black skirt, one hundred percent siren when combined with her long, lithe legs and a no-nonsense hip-swinging gait. She'd been shy until he'd gotten to know her, and then her gutsy and ambitious side had peeked through and reeled him in. Lynn dreamed big—something they had in common.

He'd debated for months before asking her out because she was too young for him, but in the end he couldn't resist. They'd dated a few times, and then he'd made the second biggest mistake of his life. He'd introduced her to his brother. An extended business trip had called him out of town, and he'd returned to find Brett and Lynn married.

Move on, Riggan. You can't change the past. She chose Brett. "You'd only make minimum wage. You deserve better."

"Sawyer, I have a high school diploma and one semester of college. I'm not qualified for anything better."

"You should have finished school."

Lynn looked away, revealing beard burn on the delicate skin of her neck. He'd marked her in his passion. The unexpected urge to soothe her chafed skin with his mouth hit him hard. "Brett wanted me here."

That wasn't the way Brett told the story. "Have you gone over the finances with your accountant yet?"

"Brett kept our books."

His belly sank even lower. Brett was a marketing genius, but numbers had never been his strong suit. "When will you meet with the lawyer to go over the will? You need to know if you have enough money to hold on to the house and your car."

She pressed a hand to her temple and bowed her head. He wanted to smooth her tangled hair as badly as he wanted his next breath. He shoved his hands deeper into his pockets. "I'll meet with the lawyer in a few days, but I've looked over the accounts. Money is going to be tight until I sell the house."

Her words didn't make sense. Brett had earned a generous salary as marketing director of Riggan CyberQuest. "You're selling the house?"

She lifted her chin and met his gaze. The wariness and fear in her eyes knotted his gut. "It's too big for just me."

He cursed his brother. If Brett had kept up the life insurance policy then Lynn wouldn't be forced to sell the house where she and Brett had lived—he swallowed hard—and loved. "What can I do to help?"

"Nothing, thanks. I've already contacted a real estate agent. He's coming out to give me an appraisal." She seemed determined to tough it out alone.

He was just as determined to help her. Lynn was his responsibility now—especially if she carried a Riggan baby in her belly. "You can move in with me until you find a new place."

Her eyes rounded. "I...no, thank you."

He couldn't blame her, since he'd violated her trust today. He shoved a hand through his hair. "What happened today... I can't tell you how much I regret it. I won't lose control again. You have my word, Lynn."

Why did the words feel like a lie? And why did Lynn flinch as if he'd slapped her? He wanted to kick himself. Instead, he pulled out his wallet and extracted the cash inside. "This is all I have with me, but I can get more—as much as you need."

She recoiled, and her skin flushed. "Are you trying to make me feel like a hooker?"

He winced and his skin heated. "No." *Dammit.* "I thought you might need money for food or...whatever."

She made no move to take the cash. "The neighbors brought enough food to last a week. I don't need anything else."

"I want to help—"

"I know you're used to taking care of Brett, but I'm twenty-three years old, Sawyer. I can take care of myself. Now I'm exhausted, so I hope you'll excuse me." She opened the front door. Her invitation to leave couldn't have been clearer.

"Lynn—"

"*Please,* Sawyer, I just can't do this right now. Go home."

She looked ready to collapse, so he didn't argue. "We're not finished."

Two

"You're saying the situation is worse than I thought?" Lynn perched on the edge of her chair across from Mr. Allen, the estate lawyer. Her nails dug into her palms, and her stomach clenched into a tight knot. An hour's worth of legal terminology spun in a confusing mass in her head.

The older gentleman regarded her somberly through his wire-rimmed bifocals from across his wide cherry desk. The richly furnished office smelled like money. Ironically, he'd just told her she had none.

"Your husband's estate is heavily burdened with debt, Mrs. Riggan. You'll have to liquidate your assets to cover those debts. As far as I can ascertain the thirty-percent share of Riggan CyberQuest you've inherited is your only debt-free asset."

Lynn gulped her rising panic and stiffened her spine. "So I should sell Brett's share of the company?"

"Yes, if you hope to have anything to live off, but your brother-in-law has right of first refusal should you choose to sell."

"That shouldn't be a problem. Sawyer will want to buy Brett's share."

Mr. Allen shuffled the papers in front of him until she thought her nerves would snap. "You have rights of survivorship on your home which means you can sell it without waiting for the estate to be settled, and I would highly recommend you do so before the bank takes action, since your payments are past due. I'll have my secretary give you the names of several reputable estate appraisers. You can have your household items assessed and then choose one of the estate men to help you divest yourself of anything of value."

She clenched her hands to stop their trembling and nodded. The tasks ahead seemed insurmountable, but Brett's share of the company should give her enough to start over and to get an education so she could support herself.

The attorney continued, "You've provided receipts showing you've paid for the funeral services, and yet the money wasn't withdrawn from any of your bank accounts."

Lynn twisted her plain gold wedding band around her finger. "No, I returned a gift my husband had recently bought…for me and used that money."

If second thoughts about their reconciliation hadn't driven her from the bed after their intimate encounter would she have ever known about Brett's mistress?

She'd picked up her husband's suit from the floor the way she'd done dozens of times before, but this time a jewelry box had fallen from his coat pocket and sprung open to reveal a huge diamond ring. She'd been touched—not because she'd liked the gaudy ring, but because she'd believed the gift signified a new start to their troubled marriage. The inscription inside the platinum band had crushed her hopes. "To Nina with love, Brett." At that moment her worst fears had been proven. Her husband had been unfaithful.

Stunned, she'd looked at Brett, and he'd concocted a story—he always had a story—about buying the ring for her and then deciding it wasn't her style. He'd claimed he planned to return it the next day and had even produced the receipt to prove his point. The worst part was that she probably would have swallowed his lies *again* if she hadn't read the inscription. He claimed the jeweler had made a mistake, but she knew better. Finally, the rose-colored glasses had shattered, and she could see the lie in his eyes.

If she hadn't been so angered by her own gullibility and lashed out at him verbally, egged on by years of broken dreams, would he still be alive? She'd screamed at him to get out of the house, vowing to file the divorce papers the next day. He'd stormed out, and less than an hour later the police had knocked on her door to tell her Brett was dead.

When it had become clear that there wasn't any money to pay for the funeral, she'd returned the ring to the jeweler's. His mistress's ring had cost more than ten thousand dollars. Her own ring, a plain gold band, had cost one hundred, which only went to show how much he valued her.

How had she been so blind? So stupid?

"Mrs. Riggan?" Mr. Allen's quiet voice interrupted her self-castigation.

She jerked to attention. "Yes?"

"I have one more suggestion. Seek employment as soon as possible."

Lynn had ducked him for the last time. He would see her today, dammit.

Sawyer ground his teeth and navigated through the congestion in Lynn and Brett's normally quiet neighborhood on Saturday morning. During the past week he'd left enough messages on Lynn's answering machine to fill a book. Sure, she'd returned his calls, but she'd left brief messages on his home answering machine when she knew he'd be at work, rather than call him at the office and speak to him directly.

How could he take care of her if he couldn't even talk to her and find out what she needed?

He'd given her time because the memory of her taste, of the slick heat of her body clenching his and her gasps of passion still haunted his dreams, but he wasn't going to let her get away with avoiding him any longer.

He turned onto her street, and traffic slowed to a crawl. The For Sale sign by the curb jolted him, but the Yard Sale sign sent his heart slamming against his ribs.

His brother's belongings lay scattered across the lawn and driveway. Scavengers hunted through the entrails of Brett's life. Rage boiled in Sawyer's chest. Brett had only been gone ten days, and Lynn seemed determined to erase his existence.

Pulling into a spot by the curb, Sawyer threw open his car door and stalked toward Lynn. Her pale-yellow shorts and sleeveless sweater skimmed her curves in a way guaranteed to make any red-blooded male stand up and take notice. Her bare arms and legs were sleek, tanned and toned, and the V-neck of her sweater revealed a mouthwatering hint of cleavage. Her hair cascaded down her back like polished gold, and she'd outlined her mouth in deep pink—the same shade he'd kissed off her lips. His libido stirred, but right now his anger edged out his primeval response by a slim margin.

She glanced up from her cash box and their gazes met. Wariness filled her eyes.

"What are you doing?" He managed not to shout, but fury vibrated in his voice.

Her white teeth dug into her bottom lip. "I'm selling items I won't have room for when I move to a smaller place."

"Those are Brett's books, his golf clubs, *his clothes.*"

"Sawyer, I'm sorry. I should have warned you about the yard sale."

"Hell, you have everything he owned out here." He fought the urge to sweep it all up and carry it back into the house.

Lynn winced and glanced over her shoulder, making him aware that several shoppers had stopped to eavesdrop shamelessly. Catching her elbow, he ushered her to the side of the lawn.

She focused soft, sympathetic eyes on him. "I separated out the items I thought you might want, but if you see anything out here that you'd like, then please, take it."

"That's not the point. It's as if you're trying to erase Brett from your memory." He wasn't ready to let go yet, and she shouldn't be, either. She pulled her arm free, and her silky skin slid against his fingertips, marginally deflating his anger. He shoved his hands in the pockets of his shorts and clenched his teeth on the persistent bite of desire.

"My memories are here, Sawyer." She tapped her

temple and then gestured toward the bounty in her yard. "These are just *things.*"

He paced to the hedge and back. Was Lynn trying to purge Brett from her life? And what if there were a child? He might have a legal hold on his child, but not on Brett's. The big aching void where his heart used to be threatened to suck him into a black hole. "Why are you trying so hard to forget him?"

"I'm not," she fired back defensively and then chewed her lip. She glanced away and then back at him. Resignation settled over her features. "We have a few debts I need to pay."

He zeroed in on the tension in her voice. "What kinds of debts?"

She stepped from one foot to the other and fingered the lock on the cash box. "It's nothing I can't handle."

"Lynn, I can't help if I don't know what I'm up against."

"And I told you I don't need your help." She fidgeted when he stared her down and then sighed. "Credit cards, mostly, but as administrator of the estate, *I* can settle our debts by selling a few items."

Hadn't Brett learned anything from the tightly budgeted years after their parents' deaths? Or was Lynn the one who'd insisted on flashy cars and a luxurious house? Since marrying his brother she'd certainly developed a high-maintenance lifestyle with her flirty body-hugging dresses, long, manicured nails and hair color that changed as frequently as the seasons.

His gut knotted and a sour taste filled his mouth. Brett had bragged that every time Lynn dyed her hair it had been like making love with a different woman, a sexy redhead, a sultry brunette, a tawny-headed temptress. Cheating, but not cheating, he'd said with a wink and a smirk that lit a firestorm in Sawyer every time. He'd once thought he and Lynn had a future together, but that was before she'd ignored his letter and chosen his brother.

Sawyer preferred Lynn's hair blond—which he now knew was her natural shade, dammit—and he'd liked her back when she'd been a waitress who traded her contradictory uniform for jeans after work. Sure, he appreciated the curvy shape her clothes revealed—what man wouldn't?—but he preferred a woman to leave a little to the imagination.

She tucked a lock of hair behind her ear with a long fuchsia fingernail, and in the blink of an eye his mind shifted gears again and his blood ignited. The crescent marks on his butt where she'd clutched him and pulled him deeper had barely faded. He cleared his throat and shifted, trying to ease the discomfort behind his zipper. "How much do you owe?"

Her pink lips pressed in a determined line, and she lifted her chin. "I'm busy now. Can we have this discussion later?"

Several couples hovered as if waiting to make purchases, and Lynn's closed expression made it clear she wasn't going to talk now. He didn't have the right to stop the yard sale, but he couldn't stand around and watch the vultures cart off his brother's possessions without acid eating a hole through his stomach. "What time will you finish here?"

"The neighbors' teenage sons will come back at three to help me pack up what I don't sell."

"I'll be back this evening."

Pretend it didn't happen. Pretend the man striding up your driveway didn't give you more physical pleasure in five desperate minutes than your husband did in four years.

Lynn hovered on her side porch with her cheeks on fire and her insides a jumble. Coward that she was, she'd anxiously watched for Sawyer through the windows and then raced out the kitchen door before he could head up the brick walk to her front entrance. She couldn't face him in the foyer.

Sawyer's navy-blue polo shirt delineated his muscles to mouthwatering perfection. The short sleeves revealed thick biceps and tanned forearms lightly sprinkled with dark hair—hair that matched the denser whorls at the base of his throat. Her lips tingled with the memory of tasting him there, and a shiver slipped down her spine. His khaki shorts displayed rock-hard thighs and calves. Dark stubble shadowed his jaw. She clenched her fingers as she relived the rasp of his chin against her palm.

She'd just lost her husband, and even if she'd quit loving Brett long ago, she shouldn't be having womb-tightening thoughts about Sawyer or his athletic body. Ashamed, she ducked her chin, thumbed her wedding band and hoped the warmth beneath her skin wasn't visible.

"You've been avoiding me," he stated without preamble.

Her heart jumped. Guilty as charged. "I've been busy for the past week with the estate paperwork, the real estate agent and appraisers."

His cobalt gaze raked over her from head to toe, stirring up feelings best left undisturbed and leaving a trail of goose bumps in its wake, but then concern softened his eyes and the hard planes of his handsome face. "How are you holding up?"

His quiet question put a lump in her throat. "I'm okay. You?"

He shrugged and she nearly rolled her eyes. Typical man, refusing to admit to emotion. Her father, the tough cop, had been the same—especially after her mother died.

"Come in." She led the way through the garage and into the kitchen. Even though she kept her back to the curved archway leading to the foyer her heart thumped harder, and the sensitive areas of her body tingled with awareness for the man hovering a few feet away.

She concentrated on keeping her hand steady so she wouldn't scatter the coffee grounds across the granite countertop and then poured water into the coffeemaker and turned it on. Pressing her palm against her nervous stomach, she tried to ignore the tremor running through her. "The coffee should be ready in a few minutes."

"How much do you owe?" Sawyer's tone sounded level, almost impersonal, but the way he looked at her wasn't. His eyes stroked over her, and her skin reacted as if he'd touched her. Intimacy stood between them like a living, breathing being, connecting them in a way they hadn't been linked before.

Don't fool yourself, Lynn. The encounter in the foyer ten days ago had nothing to do with making love and everything to do with forgetting. The regret on both sides proved it shouldn't and wouldn't be repeated. So why couldn't she get it out of her mind? And why, when he looked at her in that slow, thorough way did her awakened body hum with the memory of the way he'd caressed her and with the deep-seated need for him to do so again?

My God, what must he think of her? Had she become the clichéd merry widow? Embarrassment scorched her cheeks. She staggered back a step and retreated to the sunny bay window overlooking her tiny backyard in an effort to clear the unsuitable thoughts from her mind. She fussed with her multitude of plants, polishing dust off this one and plucking a dead bud from another, but Sawyer's spicy scent pursued her relentlessly.

"How much, Lynn?" he repeated.

"Settling the estate really isn't your problem, Sawyer."

He leaned forward, bracing his arms on the table. His biceps bulged and a muscle jerked in the tense line of his jaw. "It's my problem if you have to sell part of the company to cover your debts."

"Actually, I want to sell Brett's share back to you."

He frowned and shoved a hand through his hair. "I can't raise the capital to buy Brett's share right now. The company's having a few difficulties."

A chill chased down her spine. Those shares were all she had. If the company folded they'd be worthless. "But I need the money to start over once the house sells."

"And I need you to be patient. Give me a chance to turn the company around. You'd only get a fraction of the value if you sold now. Where do you plan to move?"

Lynn pressed her fingers against the steady throb building behind her left temple. "My aunt said I could stay with her until I get back on my feet."

"In Florida? If you're looking for a rent-free place to stay, then move in with me. I have the space."

His offer tempted and repelled her simultaneously. She loved this small college town with its steep hills, curvy roads and friendly atmosphere, and Sawyer's spacious home in the historic section had a character and grace that her newer one lacked. When he finished the renovations his house would be gorgeous. She loved the high-ceilinged rooms and tall windows which overlooked a huge yard.

But Sawyer had made her lose control, and she'd just spent four years of her life in a relationship that rendered her powerless. If she lived with him she ran the risk of repeating her mistakes. "Thanks, but let's hope it doesn't come to that."

"Are you looking for a job?"

"Yes." She'd been job hunting for the past three days, but the university students had left town for the summer, and the business owners had cut staff to accommodate reduced trade.

"Come to work for me."

With her stomach churning, she gazed out the window. The last thing she wanted to do was face Sawyer every day and be reminded that she'd thrown herself at him like a woman starved for affection. "I don't know anything about computer software development."

Sawyer moved closer until he stood directly behind her, his reflection showing in the glass. He put a hand on her shoulder and turned her to face him. The heat of his touch permeated her thin sweater, warming her skin. She swallowed hard and lifted her gaze to his. In his eyes she saw sympathy, frustration and heat. He hadn't forgotten what happened any more than she had. There beneath the civilized veneer lay the awareness of what they'd done. Tension spiraled in her belly.

"Lynn, I can give you enough money to cover your immediate expenses, or I can offer you a job. Your choice. But I don't want you to leave Chapel Hill until I'm certain you're not carrying Brett's child…or mine."

Sawyer's baby. Her pulse skipped a beat. She took a

calming breath. It would be one thing to move to Florida alone or with Brett's baby. It would be another to take Sawyer's baby away from him. She could never be responsible for denying a child its father's love.

Don't panic about things that haven't happened yet. You may not be pregnant. The odds for conceiving the first month after getting off the Pill are slim.

"Thank you, but I'd rather earn the money legitimately." She forced herself to look into his eyes and stretched her lips into a smile that felt more like a grimace, but she couldn't do any better with the worry building inside her. Stepping away, she put enough distance between them that she couldn't feel his body heat and wouldn't be close enough to give in to the temptation to lean on him and draw from his strength. It was time she stood on her own feet again.

"I want to help." His voice hardened.

She took a deep breath and faced him. "And I want a *real* job, not one fabricated out of pity."

"This is a real job. Opal, my administrative assistant, needs help. Brett's assistant quit months ago, and Opal's been juggling her workload and Nina's, too."

Lynn's breath caught and nausea rose in her throat. *Nina.* Brett's lover. Her husband went through assistants like most men went through socks. Because he'd instructed her not to call him at work unless there was an emergency, she hadn't even known his latest assistant's name. Did Sawyer know about the affair? Would he lie to protect his brother?

With her heart and head reeling she tried to come up with a logical response. "I have no training."

"You'll learn." The set of Sawyer's jaw promised an argument if she refused his offer—an argument she couldn't contemplate right now.

"I'll think about it. Now, please have a seat at the table. I have something to show you. I have to get it from the bedroom upstairs."

His gaze locked with hers and then shifted to the archway beyond her shoulder—the one leading to the foyer and the stairs. Heat flashed in his eyes.

Her breath caught and her heart pounded. Warmth flushed her skin. She turned away, but not before regret tightened Sawyer's features. "I'll get the box."

After bracing himself, Sawyer lifted the lid of the cheap wooden box on the table in front of him. Gold, silver and other precious metals lay jumbled together without regard for the scratches the heirlooms might receive.

"Did you pack these?"

Lynn hovered near the coffeepot. Her gaze danced to his and then away again, never holding for more than a split second. Pink climbed from her neck to spread across her cheeks. Her nipples peaked, proving she remembered what happened on the other side of that archway, the same way he did. His pulse leaped. Her quick glances told him she wanted to ignore the passion between them, and if he were half as smart as the business magazines said he was, he'd let her.

"I didn't even know Brett had this treasure chest until I searched for the will. I found the box buried in the back of the closet, but I saw your name on a couple of items and thought you might be interested. I'd hate to sell something that holds sentimental value for you."

She flitted from one side of the blinding-white kitchen to the other and back again—probably afraid he'd jump her if she remained stationary. She fiddled with her plants and straightened the already straight row of canisters. He cursed himself. His loss of control had made her a nervous wreck.

"You never found a will?"

"No. The attorney checked the courthouse, the bank and every other logical place where a will could be stored, just in case Brett had done one of those home kits. He found nothing, and I've already searched the house twice."

Another detail his brother had neglected. It infuriated Sawyer that Brett had been so careless with Lynn. If a man loved a woman, he looked out for her, provided for her...and any children they might have.

Shutting down the disturbing thought, he carefully withdrew a gold watch and chain from the tangled mess in the box and traced his finger over the name engraved in the metal. Warm memories swamped him—memories of looking at this watch with his own father and anticipating the day when he would be entrusted with the heirloom. "This pocket watch belonged to my great-grandfather, the first Sawyer Riggan."

She set a mug of steaming coffee in front of him and darted back to the other side of the room. "Why did Brett have it?"

"He asked for it." And God help him, he'd tried to give Brett everything he wanted after their parents' deaths.

"But why give it to him if it was intended for you?"

"I owed him." Owed him a debt he could never repay.

"Owed him what?"

Hadn't Brett told her? "I killed our parents."

Her brow pleated. "Your parents died in a car accident."

"With me at the wheel."

Sympathy softened her eyes. "I thought a drunk driver ran a stop light."

"He did, but if I hadn't shot off as soon as the light turned green, if I'd looked twice before accelerating into the intersection instead of being the lead-foot my dad always accused me of being—"

She returned to the table, slid into the chair at a right angle to his and laid her soft hand over his clenched fist. His words dried up. "Sawyer, the accident wasn't your fault. Brett showed me the newspaper article. The other driver didn't have on his headlights. You couldn't possibly have seen him."

Her touch burned his skin. He sucked in a deep breath. She snatched her hand back and tucked it into her lap as if she regretted the gesture, but the imprint of her fingers lingered.

Since Brett's death Lynn had quit wearing her heavy perfume, and God help him, he could smell *her.* Her light honeysuckle scent was ten times more potent than perfume anyday. She'd also quit teasing her hair into that just-out-of-bed, sex-kitten style. Today she'd brushed it in a satiny wave over her shoulders. His hands itched to tumble her hair into the same disarray it had been when he'd made love to her on the stairs. Not made love, he corrected, had sex. Making love implied he had lingering feelings for Lynn from their earlier relationship, and he didn't.

Clearing his throat, he refocused on the jewelry box, digging around until he uncovered his mother and father's wedding bands. He closed his fingers around them, feeling the loss of his parents as if it had been yesterday instead of ten years ago, and then his mother's last words rang in his ears. *Take care of Brett. Whatever you do, don't let them separate our family.*

He opened his hand to study the intricately carved bands and traced the pattern on his mother's ring.

Lynn leaned closer. "They're lovely. The engraving is quite unusual."

"Brett said you refused to wear Mom's wedding band."

Lynn's brows arched in surprise. "I never saw the rings before this week."

He lifted the smaller band. "He didn't offer this to you?"

Pain clouded her sky-blue eyes and she looked away. "No. Maybe he wanted to keep the set together. You know Brett chose not to wear a wedding band."

It didn't make sense. Brett had begged for the pocket watch and the rings, and yet it would seem his brother had never used any of the pieces.

A delicate silver locket caught Sawyer's attention. He set the rings back in the box and picked up the locket, flicking it open to reveal two tiny pictures, one of him as an infant and the other of Brett as a three-year-old. "This belonged to my mother. She always planned to give it to her granddaughter, if there was one someday."

His gaze met hers and then traveled slowly over her breasts to her flat belly. His child—his daughter—could be growing inside Lynn. His chest tightened, and he lifted his gaze to hers once more. She worried her bottom lip with her teeth. Her lipstick was long gone. The need to lean across the distance and touch his mouth to the softness of hers blindsided him. He sucked in a slow breath and sat back in his chair.

Neither of them spoke of the baby she might be carrying, but the knowledge and the tension stretched between them. He couldn't explain the mixture of emotions clogging his throat. Fear? Excitement? Dread? Anticipation?

Lynn's fingers curled on the edge of the tabletop until her knuckles turned white, and then she stood and carried her cup to the sink. "If you ever have a daughter, I'm sure she'd be proud to wear the locket. It's lovely."

The other items in the box held less value, but Sawyer found a favorite pocket knife he thought he'd lost in high school and the ID bracelet his ex-fiancée had given him. Why did Brett have these? And why had he tossed each piece in a cheap box like yard-sale junk?

Lynn paused behind his shoulder. "These are your memories, Sawyer. They should stay in your family."

"The Riggan family will end with me—unless you're carrying the next generation. When will you know if you're pregnant?"

Eyes wide, she stared at him and then her gaze darted away. Her face paled as quickly as it had flushed. "In a week or so, but let's not borrow trouble."

"You'll tell me as soon as you know." It wasn't a question.

She hesitated and his heart stuttered. "Yes."

"Do you want a baby?"

Worry clouded her eyes. She took a deep breath. "I've always wanted children, but the timing couldn't be worse. And not knowing who—" She bit her lip and tucked her chin.

"I'll stand by you, Lynn—no matter whose child it is."

"Um…thank you." She didn't look reassured.

The doorbell rang. She frowned and turned.

"That should be dinner. I called the Chinese place while you were upstairs." Sawyer rose and strode past her to the front door. She remained in the kitchen while he paid and tipped the delivery man and returned. He set the bag on the counter and opened it. Tantalizing aromas filled the room.

"You didn't have to buy dinner." Lynn inhaled deeply and then licked her lips.

Hunger for Lynn replaced his need for food. He gritted his teeth and reminded himself why he'd called the restaurant. "You need to eat. You've lost weight."

Her spine stiffened. "That's not your concern."

"I'm making it mine."

Three

A polished woman in her fifties guarded the closed door with Sawyer Riggan, CEO, engraved on the nameplate.

Lynn swallowed her nervousness and crossed the threshold of the office. "Excuse me. I'm Lynn Riggan. I'd like to see Sawyer."

The woman's frank appraisal made Lynn want to fidget. She clutched her purse tighter when what she really wanted to do was smooth her French twist and straighten the skirt of her fitted emerald-green dress. She shifted her weight in her three-inch heels, hating the clothes Brett had chosen for her, but until she could afford to replace them she was stuck.

The woman rose. "I'm Opal Pugh, Sawyer's assistant. I'm sorry for your loss, Mrs. Riggan."

"Thank you. It's nice to meet you, Opal." This was

the woman Brett had referred to as Sawyer's dragon lady.

"I'll see if Sawyer's free." Opal tapped on Sawyer's door before disappearing inside.

Lynn hated depending on Sawyer for a job, but everywhere she'd gone the answers had been the same. Not hiring. Twisting the strap of her purse, she examined the tastefully decorated office. Thick steel-gray carpeting covered the floor. An oak coffee table gleamed in front of a burgundy-damask-covered loveseat and chairs, and the landscapes on the wall looked like originals.

Before she could step nearer to read the artists' signatures, the door opened and her stomach dropped. Opal motioned her forward. "He'll see you now."

Lynn's legs trembled as she closed the distance. She wished she could blame her fluttery nerves and agitated stomach solely on her dismal financial situation, but the man rising from behind the wide oak desk in front of her contributed more than a little. Sawyer seemed larger than life here on his own turf—every inch a mastermind who'd taken an idea and turned it into an internationally renowned company. He'd shed his suit coat and rolled up the sleeves of his white dress shirt. The loosened knot of his tie and opened top two buttons of his shirt revealed a glimpse of his dark chest hair.

"Good morning, Lynn." His baritone voice sounded deeper than usual. It skipped down her spine like a caress. His intense blue eyes glided over her slowly, thoroughly assessing her.

"Good morning." Her dry mouth made it difficult to form the words. She cursed the heat flaring in her face and other places she'd rather not acknowledge and tugged at her dress. She'd always tried to ignore her clingy clothing, but after her steamy dreams last night—dreams featuring Sawyer—her skin was hypersensitive to the brush of the fabric against her breasts, hips and thighs.

With a subtle lift of his square chin, he motioned for Opal to leave them. The door closed and the room suddenly seemed smaller, more intimate. Airless. She cleared her throat. "I've decided to take you up on the job offer…if it's still open."

"Certainly. Welcome aboard." Leaning across the desk, he offered his hand.

If she could have thought of a polite way to avoid the handshake, she would have. Instead, his long fingers closed around hers. She tried to focus on something besides the memory of how those warm, long-fingered hands had cradled her bottom while he thrust deep inside her, first in her foyer and then again in her dreams last night.

A hint of his spicy aftershave teased her senses, and an image of his passion-glazed eyes flashed in her brain. Her heart jolted into a faster rhythm, and her cheeks weren't the only parts of her that were growing warm. Brett had accused her of being a prude, but her thoughts certainly weren't prudish now.

She pulled her hand free and blurted, "I need to make it clear that I'm only looking for a job…not anything else."

He reared back. The nostrils of his straight nose flared, and she cringed with embarrassment. "I'm sorry. That was—"

"We agreed that what happened was a mistake." He gestured for her to take a seat in one of the leather chairs in front of his desk.

Feeling utterly foolish, she collapsed into the visitor's seat. Of course he didn't want more of her. No man did.

"And your job here will never be based on...fringe benefits, but you're a co-owner of the business, so we will be working closely together. Will that be a problem for you?"

Would it be a problem to work beside him every single day? Yes. "No."

Sawyer settled in his chair behind the wide desk and laced his fingers on the polished surface. "When would you like to start?"

She swallowed to ease the dryness in her mouth. "Today? Tomorrow? But first, I'd like a little time in Brett's office...if that's okay?"

Sympathy filled his eyes, and she felt like a fraud. She wasn't a brokenhearted widow. She'd done her share of grieving over her marriage months ago. Now she just felt foolish for having wasted more than four years of her life on what had obviously been a losing proposition.

"You know where it is?"

"I think so." Brett had rarely brought her to the office and never during regular business hours.

She walked down the short hall on shaky legs and into her husband's office. She didn't have to turn to know that Sawyer had followed. Her personal radar was keenly attuned to his presence just one stride behind.

He reached around her to lift a crystal picture frame from the desktop and his shoulder brushed hers. Her breath hitched and her skin prickled at the point of contact. "I've asked Opal to bring in some boxes. You'll want to take Brett's personal items home—including this."

She took the picture from him and stared at the

blond-haired and blue-eyed couple as if they were strangers instead of Brett and herself. Her eyes glowed and she smiled as if someone had just handed her the world on a platter. How long had it been since she'd felt even a fraction of that hope and happiness? But she'd believed in her marriage vows, and she'd tried to make the relationship work.

Why hadn't she noticed before that the emotion captured in her husband's eyes wasn't love, but possessiveness? How stupid of her not to realize sooner that she'd been nothing but an accessory to Brett. He'd expected her to dress to suit his tastes, to maintain the perfect house and image, to be seen and not heard. But why her? His journal made it clear he hadn't been motivated by love.

The warmth of Sawyer's hand on her shoulder jerked her attention back to the concern and sadness in his eyes. Not for the first time she noted the difference between the two men. Brett's eyes were pale blue and his hair sandy blond. Sawyer's eyes were intensely deep blue, shades darker than Brett's, and his hair was raven's-wing black.

Right now he was frowning at her. "Are you all right? Would you like for me to have someone else handle the packing?"

"I can do it. I'm okay," she lied, and stepped away, but her skin tingled where he'd touched, and the urge to lean on his broad shoulders nearly overpowered her.

Looking back on it now, she realized she hadn't been okay since the second year of her marriage when her husband had started systematically eroding her self-confidence. He'd begun with suggesting she dye her hair a more attractive color and then he'd progressed to urging her to get breast implants and collagen in her lips. She'd refused the medical procedures but she'd experimented with hair colors. None had satisfied him, and she'd recently returned to her natural blond.

She'd wanted so desperately to have the family Brett had promised her before they married, wanted so very much to please him and to turn him back into the man who'd charmed her right out of her disappointment over the end of her relationship with Sawyer. She'd failed on all counts.

She shook off her depressing thoughts. "Could I have a few minutes alone?"

"Of course. I've spent some time in here myself." The pain in Sawyer's voice made her heart ache. She wanted to reach for him but didn't. With obvious reluctance he backed toward the door. "My extension's marked on the phone. Ring if you need anything."

As soon as the door closed, Lynn lay the photo face-down on the desktop and stepped behind the polished surface. She rifled through the drawers, but she didn't know what she was looking for. Additional bank accounts? Signs of Brett's infidelity? A tap on the door made her jump guiltily. She closed the drawer. "Yes?"

Opal stepped inside with an armload of boxes, which she set in the visitor's chair. "Would you like some help packing?"

"No, thank you."

"Sawyer says you want a job. What can you do?" The woman's cool tone and expression implied she wasn't overly thrilled to have Lynn's assistance foisted upon her. Lynn's heart sank. What could she do besides wait tables and plan elaborate dinner parties?

"I helped Brett whenever he brought work home. I can type. And I—" She bit her lip, hesitant to admit she'd baby-sat for the neighbors' children on the sly for spending money, and then she'd sneaked out to take classes at the local technical college without Brett's knowledge. But Brett was gone. Her secrets couldn't hurt her anymore. ''I've also taken a few computer classes at Orange Tech.''

Opal's eyes narrowed speculatively and then she moved around the desk and booted up the computer. ''That's a start. Let's see how many of the computer programs you recognize.''

Familiar icons appeared on the screen and the tension eased from Lynn's shoulders. She could do this. ''I've used most of these before.''

''Honey, it would be my lucky day if you knew anything about designing promotional brochures. That's what Brett was working on before the accident.'' Opal shoved her glasses into her graying hair. ''I don't know much about graphics, but the project has landed on my desk. I have to finish it or farm it out.''

Lynn smiled at the dread in Opal's voice. ''Brett worked on the flyer at home on his laptop. He struggled with the software when Sawyer bought it last year. I read the instruction manual while Brett was at work and did the tutorial exercises so that I could demonstrate the program to him.'' She hesitated and then confessed. ''I took a class in the software program last fall.''

Opal's penciled brows rose. ''Are you willing to take a stab at laying out the brochure? It would save us the expense of hiring an outside company.''

What did she have to lose? ''I can try.''

''Great. Do what you can and then we'll run it by Sawyer. Would it be too difficult for you to work in here? The files are already on this computer.''

''This is fine.'' If she worked hard at it she could probably forget Sawyer was only two doors down.

* * *

"I don't want the Feds in on this, Carter." Sawyer faced his former college roommate across the table in the basement restaurant that had once been their college hangout. "I want to know who's been robbing my company, and I want to keep it quiet."

"No problem. You're privately owned. It's not like you're screwing stockholders by withholding information."

"My sister-in-law and I are the only owners, but I'd rather Lynn not catch wind of the investigation. She has enough on her plate without having to worry about the business going under."

"Yeah, man, sorry about Brett." Carter fingered the paper coaster under his beer. "Do you think it's an inside job?"

Sawyer tried to ignore the ache in his chest that cropped up every time someone mentioned his brother's name. He rubbed the back of his neck and shook his head. "Everything I've found points in that direction, but there are only fifteen of us, and we get along. I can't picture anybody being disgruntled enough to sell company secrets. I've messed up somewhere in my tracking, or someone's laid a false trail."

"Mess up? You? I doubt it. Statistics support the theory of an insider being your leak. Internal theft is number one in the industry."

Bile burned Sawyer's throat at the thought of someone close stealing from him. He ate at his team members' houses, went boating with them on the lake and attended their weddings. They played in a company softball league together. "I trust my team."

Skepticism tightened Carter's features. "Well, it's my job to find out if that trust is misplaced. Do you want me working on the inside or hacking in from outside?''

''Are you kidding? You have quite a reputation for your cybersleuthing. The alarm would sound if you turned up in our offices. I'll grant you access.''

''Won't your team pick up another player in the field?''

''My number-one intrusion detector is on paternity leave for the next month. I'm covering for him while he's out. The rest are neck deep in a custom-designed program for a pharmaceutical company, but I'll give you my password and log-in just in case.''

''You trust me that much, huh?''

''Like a brother.''

''Back atcha.'' Carter sipped his beer. ''So how much did this cost you?''

''A bundle. We were weeks away from launching a new program, but somebody beat us to it. Worse, I suspect this wasn't the first leak. We had another incident a couple of years back. I passed it off as bad luck, but now I'm not so sure. I added the past dates to the file.''

''Will the company survive?''

Sawyer wadded his paper napkin and shoved his lasagna aside. ''It will if we can stop the leak and prevent it from happening again.''

''Like you said, I'm good at what I do. We'll get your man. In the meantime, I need the names of all your employees, and I want to know who has access to what.''

Sawyer finished his beer. ''I'll go back to the office and e-mail that to you from my private account. The place should be deserted on a Friday night.''

Carter tapped the folder on the table. ''The information in here is enough to get me started.''

"Thanks, Carter. I'll owe you."

His buddy chuckled. "Nah, man, but we might be even."

She wasn't useless, and she'd prove it. Three days was too long to struggle with this blasted brochure, and Lynn was determined to conquer it rather than have it hanging over her head all weekend.

She swallowed to alleviate the nasty taste in her mouth and resized the image on her screen for the umpteenth time. Her stomach must have finally realized that she wasn't going to break for lunch or dinner. It had quit growling hours ago, and now churned like an agitating washing machine. She should call it a night, but she was so close to finishing.

Her stomach churned harder. A trip to the water fountain might help. She rose. A wave of dizziness swept over her and a cold sweat beaded her upper lip. She had to clutch the edge of the desk for support. Oh, Lord, she couldn't afford to get sick now—not when she had to prove her worth and she hadn't yet built up any paid sick time.

Stumbling around her desk, she headed for the hall. Her stomach lurched, and she thanked her stars the offices were empty and no one would witness her undignified sprint for the ladies' room. She slammed through the door, dropped to her knees in the closest stall and retched.

The door glided open behind her. Alarm pricked the hairs on the back of her neck because the offices should be empty, but she couldn't get up.

"Lynn, are you okay? I saw you run in here."

Sawyer. She cringed and heaved. Why did the man

always find her at her worst? ‘‘Fine,’’ she mumbled and promptly made a liar of herself.

Water splashed in the sink. A long-fingered hand entered her peripheral vision a split-second before a cold paper towel touched her forehead.

Grateful, she took the towel and waved him away. He stepped back but didn’t leave the room. After what seemed like an eon, her nausea finally abated. The ridges of the cold floor tiles dug into her knees, and a draft of air from the overhead air-conditioning chilled her skin. Flushing the toilet, she slowly rose.

Her knees quivered and her head spun. She braced herself on the cool metal stall. Sawyer stepped forward, hooked an arm around her waist and guided her to the sink. She splashed water on her face, rinsed her mouth and used the paper towels he offered to dry off.

Catching her reflection in the vanity mirror, she grimaced. Not attractive. Dark mascara half-moons shadowed her eyes, and the remnants of her blush looked overly bright on her pale skin. Her blue dress accentuated the shadows under her eyes. *Charming.* She scrubbed away what she could of her ruined makeup before turning to lean her hips against the marble countertop for support.

Sawyer’s laser-sharp gaze traveled from her face to her toes and back again, making her aware of how rumpled she must look. ‘‘Are you pregnant?’’

His words stole her breath and tripped her heart. She did a quick mental calculation and her knees wobbled. Oh, Lord. With the stress of settling the estate and starting this job she hadn’t realized she was late. Or maybe she’d subconsciously blocked it out. ‘‘I don’t know.’’

‘‘I’ll drive you home. We’ll stop and pick up a pregnancy test kit on the way.’’

Alarm prickled her skin. If she was pregnant she wanted time *alone* to digest the fact and to figure out what she was going to do. ''That isn't necessary.''

''Yes, it is. You could be carrying my child.''

The wind sailed out of her. With alarm or excitement? She didn't know. ''Maybe this is just the stomach flu.''

He didn't look like he bought her flu story. The worst part was, she didn't either. With her recent run of bad luck, it was probably Brett's baby—now when she could least afford the family she'd always wanted. Or Sawyer's baby. Her stomach pitched again. She pressed a hand to her middle and mentally measured the distance back to the stall.

Sawyer yanked open the rest room door, and the gust of fresh air revived her. ''Grab your stuff and shut down your computer. When did you last eat?''

She winced and preceded him into the hall. ''Breakfast.''

His brows dipped. ''I'll get some juice and crackers from the break room for you to eat in the car. Meet me outside in three minutes.'' He issued the order as if expecting unquestioning compliance and her hackles rose.

''Sawyer—''

''Just do it, Lynn.'' His implacable tone warned her not to waste time arguing and sent an invigorating surge of adrenaline through her system. Brett had been big on issuing commands.

She did as Sawyer asked, however, building her arguments as she closed up her office, but by the time she met him in the parking lot, the jolt of angry energy had subsided, and she was too tired to insist on driving her own vehicle. She climbed into his SUV and nibbled on crackers during the short drive to the pharmacy. He instructed her to sit tight and went into the store without her to purchase the test kit. All too soon he returned.

Twenty minutes later he pulled into her driveway, killed the engine and handed her the brown paper bag. "I'll have your car delivered first thing in the morning."

"Thanks." Lethargy weighted her limbs. She did not have the energy to deal with the test tonight. All she wanted was to crawl into bed and sleep around the clock. "I'll um…see you tomorrow."

Sawyer came around and opened her door. The tension in his face mirrored the knot in her stomach. "I'm coming in."

Her fingers tightened on the bag. The crinkle of the paper seemed unusually loud. With the garage door closed, she had no option but to use the front entrance. Her hands shook as she unlocked the door. It took several tries to line the key up with the lock, but then she did and the knob turned. Sawyer followed her into the foyer. A flash of heat shot through her at the memory of that night. She couldn't look at him, couldn't bear to see the regret in his eyes. She gestured toward the living room. "Make yourself comfortable. Excuse me."

Her heels clicked across the marble floor. The bag weighed her down like lead ballast as she climbed the stairs. Sawyer's tread behind her stopped her in her tracks. She spun around and found her eyes level with his. "What are you doing?"

"I'll wait upstairs while you do the test." The determined set of his jaw and the turmoil in his eyes stifled her protest.

She turned and trudged up the remaining steps. The tension inside her coiled tighter with each riser she climbed. She entered the guest room. Not even for Sawyer's sake, could she bear being in the room she'd shared with Brett—the room where she'd been such a failure as a wife and as a woman—when she discovered whether or not she would soon be a mother.

"You've moved out of the master bedroom."

She cringed at the shock in his voice. He'd obviously noticed her personal belongings scattered about the room and her clothing through the open closet door.

"This was my parents' bedroom furniture. My grandmother made that quilt for their wedding present. I needed to be..." Unwilling to explain and be laughed at, she rolled a shoulder.

"Close to them." Sympathy and understanding shone in his eyes. Brett had never accepted her need for a link to her past. He'd wanted to throw out what he'd called her "old junk."

Her last glimpse as she closed the bathroom door was of Sawyer settling on the edge of her creaky brass bed. Stoic and determined to do the right thing, he couldn't be more unlike his brother, who'd chosen the easiest route more often than not.

The bag rattled noisily when she opened it, and she imagined Sawyer knowing every move she made by the sounds slipping through the closed door. She read the instructions once, twice, and then she unpacked the components and read the directions a third time.

Her hands shook and her queasiness returned. The pieces seemed minuscule and slippery, and her fingers had turned to thumbs. Three minutes. Two lines yes. One line no.

She followed the instructions and then washed her hands and face, brushed her teeth to fill the time and looked at her watch. Two minutes left. Keeping her eyes averted from the test stick, she combed her hair and straightened the items on her bathroom countertop. No sound came from the other side of the door. Was Sawyer as nervous about this as she?

She checked her watch. One minute left. Did she want to be pregnant?

Yes.

No.

She couldn't decide. Reason warred with emotion. She wanted a baby, but she couldn't afford one and Brett's debts, too.

Her heart pounded and perspiration dampened her skin. With her back to the test stick, she focused on the second hand of her watch and counted backward from thirty. Three. Two. One. She closed her eyes. Her feet seemed glued to the floor, and her heart lodged in her throat. Unlocking her muscles, she turned inch-by-painful inch and forced her lids open.

Two lines. Her skin flushed with joy, but then reality settled like a cold, wet blanket on her shoulders.

She was expecting a baby, but *whose?*

Four

The bathroom door opened, and Sawyer turned away from the window. He took in Lynn's shocked expression. His stomach dropped. His heart slammed against his ribs with the force and speed of a jackhammer.

"You're pregnant."

"Apparently so," she whispered.

"We'll get married," he announced without preamble. He'd run the possible scenarios over in his mind, and marriage was the best way to establish a legal connection with the child.

Her eyes widened and she clutched the door frame. Her horrified expression shredded his ego. "But the baby might not be yours."

He ground his teeth against the unexpected burn in his chest. Did it matter who'd fathered her child? This baby was the only family he had left and, dammit, he would keep his family together. ''I want to be a father to this child.''

''Sawyer, that's not necessary, and if I'm living in Florida—''

Panic clawed his throat. ''Families belong together.''

She looked trapped. A shaky breath lifted her breasts beneath the bodice of the pale blue dress the exact shade of her eyes—eyes now rounded with horror and shock. ''Well yes, but we don't have to get married. If this is your child then I'll find an apartment here in town, and you can visit as much as you like.''

''And if it's not?''

''Then I'll move in with my aunt.''

He couldn't let that happen. He'd lost Brett, but he would not lose Brett's child. ''How will you know whose baby it is before it's born without DNA testing?''

''I won't. I don't know much about prenatal DNA testing, but I think there's some risk to the baby involved. I'm not willing to jeopardize my baby when waiting a few months will give us the answer.''

At least they agreed on something. ''I want to be the second parent either way. You know one parent isn't as good as two. When we were dating you told me your life changed dramatically after your mother died.''

She didn't look convinced. ''Sawyer, you're still grieving over Brett and you're not thinking straight. One of these days you're going to want to get married and start your own family.''

''Brett would have wanted me to take care of you and the baby.''

''I don't think—''

He sliced a hand toward the pile of bills on the dresser and her protest died. ''Lynn, you're up to your eyeballs in debt. Admit it, you can't make it alone.''

"If you'd buy my share of the company, then that wouldn't be a problem."

"I told you I can't do that now, and the agreement Brett signed grants me twelve months to raise the capital."

She wrung her hands. "Can't you get a loan?"

"For a million dollars? Not without putting CyberQuest up as collateral. I won't do that."

Her mouth dropped open. She probably hadn't realized the value of Brett's share. "I don't want to get married again."

The ache in his chest that had been present since his brother's death expanded until it hurt to breathe. Losing Brett had obviously hurt her as much as it had him. He closed the distance between them, but shoved his hands in his pockets before the urge to reach for her and hold her close overwhelmed his common sense.

"I'm asking for twelve months. By that time I should be able to buy your share of the company, and we'll know who fathered this baby. Regardless of the parentage, I'll establish a trust fund for the baby when we divorce. It'll take at least a year to settle Brett's estate. In the meantime, you'd have the best health care money can buy and a roof over your head."

"You don't know what you're asking," she whispered with her anguished gaze fixed on his face.

The pressure in his chest increased. "I understand that you still love Brett. I'm not trying to replace him. I want to remember him as much as you do."

She hugged her arms around her waist and turned away. Her stiff spine and hunched shoulders clearly shouted refusal.

He wanted to pretend his ego wasn't wounded, but only a fool fooled himself. He closed the door on his emotions and focused on the facts. "North Carolina doesn't require blood tests or waiting periods, but we'll have to apply for a license. It will take about a week to get the paperwork in order. I'll need your birth certificate."

She flashed a deer-in-the-headlights stare over her shoulder.

"I've almost finished renovating another suite of rooms—a bedroom with a full bath and an adjoining sitting room. We'll make it your room and a nursery."

"A marriage without love is a miserable one."

The haunted look in her eyes and the torment in her voice made the muscles between his shoulder blades tense. He'd known her mother died when Lynn was eleven and that afterward her father had buried himself in his work and left Lynn in her maiden aunt's care, but he hadn't realized that her parents had been unhappy together.

He shrugged off his sympathy and lifted the top letter from the stack of bills. "The bank has started foreclosure proceedings against you. The house payment is sixty days past due. Brett's death might buy you a little extra time, but not much. Where will you go?"

He barely heard her gasp, but the pallor of her skin was hard to miss. "You had no business snooping though my mail."

He hadn't intended to look through her personal mail, but she'd been locked in that bathroom for the longest thirteen minutes and twenty seconds of his life, and red past-due notices were hard to miss even from across the room—especially when he was trying not to stare a hole through the bathroom door.

How could Brett let two months pass without making payments? Had Lynn run up so much credit card debt that they couldn't afford the house payment? Questions rolled through his brain, but he didn't voice them. Attacking her now would be like kicking a kitten.

He cupped her shoulders and waited until she met his gaze. "Would you rather I didn't care? Do you want me to walk out of here tonight and let the bank turn you and your baby out on the street?"

He couldn't do it, but she probably didn't know that.

The tension seeped from her shoulders until she looked tired, fragile and on the verge of tears. He wanted to hold her and promise her everything would be all right, but he couldn't, because he couldn't guarantee that he could find the slime ball who was stealing from him.

"No. I just...I don't think I can marry you."

Cripes, was marrying him a fate worse than death? Even without his promise to his mother, he wanted to take care of Lynn and the child growing inside her. He had the strangest urge to see her belly swell as the Riggan baby—whosever it was—thrived. A surge of possessiveness like he'd never before experienced shot through his veins.

"You've seen my backyard, Lynn. It's huge. We'll build a swing set and a sandbox, and you'll still have room for that vegetable garden you always wanted." He despised himself for using against her the dreams she'd told him back when they were dating, but he'd do whatever it took to hold on to this child.

He kicked his common sense to the curb and pulled her close. Though her muscles remained tense, he savored her softness and warmth against his chest, her honeysuckle scent filling his nostrils and the silken touch of her hair against his chin, his cheek. She felt right in his arms, but she shouldn't.

One taste of forbidden passion is all you're going to get, Riggan, so put a lid on it.

He put a few inches between them and waited for his heart to settle and for her to lift her gaze to his. "Marry me and let me make a home for you and your baby."

The yearning in her eyes put a lump in his throat, but it was home and family she craved, not him, and he'd better not forget it. There wasn't any love between them. Nevertheless, his heart slammed against his ribs and the urge to kiss her burned through his veins like a lit fuse. He ground his teeth against the heat in his groin and released her before he crossed the line. Again.

Lynn's knees went weak at the magnitude of what Sawyer asked. She sank down on the edge of her bed and buried her face in her hands. How could she trust another man? And not just any man, but one who would hate her if he knew she'd driven his baby brother from the house that night? No, she hadn't caused Brett's death, but she might have contributed to his reckless mood.

But how could she deny her child a father?

Did she dare risk living with Sawyer? She'd been well on the way to falling in love with him four and a half years ago when he'd taken off on a business trip. She hadn't needed a college education to recognize what it meant when a man left town without saying goodbye and didn't call or write. He hadn't wanted her. He'd found her lacking…just as Brett and her father had.

Sawyer dropped to his knees in front of her and cocooned her icy hands in his warm grasp. His steady, cobalt gaze held hers. "Lynn, I will love this child as if it were my own, no matter who the father is."

Her heart thundered so hard she could barely think.

She wanted to believe in the honest expression in his eyes, but Brett had fooled her with his false sincerity so many times that she didn't trust her own judgment anymore. Tearing her gaze away from his, she looked from the wedding band on her hand to the stack of bills on her dresser, and felt overwhelmed.

Until she'd posted the notice of Brett's death in the paper she'd had no idea how many creditors she'd inherited. Each day's mail brought a fresh stack of bills. She could only hope the money she'd raised from the yard sale and the proceeds generated by selling everything of value in the house would clear her debts. Brett's own credit card balances would eat up her salary. Living rent free appealed, but the trust fund Sawyer promised for her baby was the clincher.

Money issues aside, what if something happened to her the way it had to her mother? A simple cold had turned into fatal pneumonia. One day her mother had been full of love and life and the next, gone. Her father, while never demonstrative, had completely shut down his emotions. He'd started putting in overtime on the job, leaving Lynn hungry for any sign that her father loved her and didn't blame her for bringing home the virus that had killed her mother. Her unmarried aunt had helped out, but when the scandal broke after her father's death, her aunt made plans to move away the day Lynn turned eighteen. Lynn had felt discarded. Unloved. Unwanted.

She was determined that her child would never experience those debilitating emotions. If something happened to her, Sawyer would never neglect her baby. But could she live with another man she didn't love for the sake of her child? She bit her lip and met Sawyer's gaze. Twelve months. Surely two adults could be roommates for such a short time?

"What about sex?" Heat flared under her skin, and she wished she'd broached the subject more diplomatically.

Sawyer stilled, his gaze never straying from hers. "What about it?"

"If we're not…intimate, then how will you—" Embarrassment choked off her words. She cleared her throat and tried again. "Where will you…?"

He shot to his feet with a stunned expression on his face. "Are you asking if I'm going to cheat on you?"

Why wouldn't he? Brett had. Besides, this wouldn't be a normal marriage. She wet her lips and tried not to reveal how difficult this conversation was for her. "Would it be cheating if we're not—"

"Yes," he interjected, and then wiped a hand over his jaw and examined her suspiciously. "Are you asking permission to take lovers?"

"No!"

"Good, because I'd have a damned hard time granting it."

"But—"

"Lynn, I've never lived like a monk, and I can't claim I'm looking forward to it now, but wedding vows are sacred even if this is only for the baby, and I won't ask the preacher to drop the 'keep only unto you' part."

Ducking her head, she bit her lip. She'd believed in the sacredness of her vows once, too, but life had taught her that not everyone shared her views.

He paced to the door and back. "I can keep my pants zipped for a year. I expect you to do the same."

The hard look he shot her made her squirm, and then he dropped to one knee and recaptured her hands.

"Lynn, this is the best decision for all of us. I swear on Brett's grave that you won't regret marrying me."

Her stomach clenched. For her baby's sake she couldn't afford not to take a chance on this marriage. Wetting her lips, she said a silent prayer that she wasn't making another mistake. "I hope you're right."

He briefly closed his eyes and then stood, pulling her to her feet. "Come on. You need more than crackers for dinner."

What she needed was time alone to come to terms with her condition and to consider the ramifications of her decision, but Sawyer didn't seem willing to grant it. "I don't want to go out."

"No need. I'll cook." His fingers tangled with hers, and their palms pressed together. The intimacy stirred her already agitated nerves even more. He towed her toward the door and into the hall without releasing her hand.

"You can cook?" Brett had never helped in the kitchen.

He glanced over his shoulder as he descended the stairs and arched a dark brow. "Who do you think fed us after Mom died?"

"It would have been easier for you to let him go into foster care. You were only twenty-two."

He turned, leaving her on the step where she'd sat with him buried inside her. Her thighs trembled and her lungs felt tight. "Sometimes the easy way isn't the right one."

"And sometimes the right one isn't easy. You're rushing me, Sawyer. I need space."

"And our baby needs food. From now on, it's my job to take care of both of you."

* * *

Sawyer was back from his meeting. Lynn parked her car in the space next to his and made her way into the Riggan CyberQuest offices on Monday afternoon. She pressed a hand to her nervous stomach and prayed her lunch would stay put.

Surprise brought her to a halt inside her office door. Someone had placed a tiny refrigerator in the corner of her office during her lunch break. She opened it and found the inside had been stocked with yogurt, juices and bottled water. A colorful bowl on top of the unit held a variety of crackers plus a selection of fresh fruit.

She continued behind her desk, sat in the stiff leather chair and stored her purse in the bottom drawer. Sawyer's bold handwriting on her blotter caught her eye. ''Don't skip meals.'' Her hackles rose at the command. Sawyer was taking his guardian job to the limit, but he had the baby's best interest in mind, and a caring father was exactly what she wanted for her child.

She'd spent most of the weekend trying without luck to devise an alternative to marriage. Sawyer didn't want a wife any more than she wanted a husband. He only wanted access to the child, and the legalities of that should be easy enough to arrange. But this was an open-minded university town. They could share the baby and a home without getting married, couldn't they?

Opal tapped on the door and entered. ''Congratulations on your engagement and your pregnancy. I have three children and two grandchildren. Feel free to ask me any questions you have about the pregnancy.''

Dumbfounded at the abrupt statement and feeling somewhat trapped, Lynn blinked, inhaled a shaky breath and sank bonelessly back into her chair. How could she break the engagement if Sawyer had already announced both it and her condition to his staff? And if she refused to marry him, would she still have a job? Sawyer couldn't fire a partial owner of the company, could he? But he could make her life a living hell, and she refused to put herself through that again. She'd had enough of feeling unwanted, inadequate and in the way.

"Lynn, Sawyer will take good care of you and the baby. He's a wonderful man, and I'm sure he'll make a wonderful father. I've never known anyone more loyal to his family, friends and staff—even when he shouldn't be." Opal bent her head and busied herself with filing papers in the wooden file cabinet.

The hair on Lynn's nape prickled. Did Opal know about Brett's affair? Did everyone in the office know? Embarrassment scorched her cheeks.

Opal closed the drawer. "Sawyer wants to see you as soon as you get settled."

The butterflies in Lynn's stomach took flight. She rose and wiped her palms over her hips. "Tell him I'll be right there."

"Certainly. By the way, I like your dress. That classic style is flattering."

"Thank you." She loved the way her nearly new navy-blue dress skimmed her curves instead of clinging. If only she could get rid of the stiletto heels as easily, but the shop hadn't had any shoes in her size.

Opal left and Lynn followed her into the hall. What would Sawyer think of the new Lynn, the one who'd traded in her provocative clothing at the local consignment shop for a less revealing wardrobe? Why did she care? She'd wasted four years of her life trying to please a man. The only approval she needed to earn from Sawyer was for her work.

Opal motioned for her to go ahead into Sawyer's office. Lynn paused on the threshold, heart in her throat. The man was stable, successful and gorgeous. He could have any woman he wanted. Why—other than the child she carried—would he settle for her?

Sawyer's attention didn't waver from his computer screen. She took the opportunity to study him. A dark lock of hair tumbled over his forehead. He'd shed his suit coat and rolled up his sleeves. His big hands moved over the keyboard with the same surety that they'd moved over her body. Her stomach tightened. She tried to suppress the unwanted thought.

"You wanted to see me?"

He jerked to face her, abruptly shut off the monitor and stood. Curiosity sparked in his eyes and then his intense gaze swept over her as thoroughly as a caress before returning to her face. "Have a seat."

Her knees trembled as she crossed the carpet to perch on a visitor's chair. "Thank you for the refrigerator and snacks, but if it's to help the morning sickness, then I didn't have any today. And, Sawyer, I'm perfectly capable of feeding myself."

"I'm sure you are. I'm just making it easier. From what staff members and friends have told me about pregnancy, morning sickness doesn't limit itself to mornings. It's supposed to help if you snack frequently." A frown puckered his forehead. "New dress?"

"Yes."

He massaged the back of his neck with one hand and paced toward the window. At the end of the room he turned and faced her. "Why don't you let me hold on to your credit cards for a while? If you find something you really need, we'll discuss it."

She gaped at him. Alarm made the fine hairs on her

skin rise. Brett had scrutinized every purchase she made. "No."

"I know you're upset over losing Brett and that shopping is supposed to be a real panacea for some women, but it would be a good idea if you didn't buy anything else until the estate's settled and you have a handle on your credit card debt."

Stunned, she continued to stare. He thought *she* was the one with the spending problem? She'd been pinching pennies her entire life. "That's an incredibly sexist comment."

He had the grace to flush, but gestured to her dress with the sweep of his hand. "You deny that you went shopping over the weekend?"

"I traded some of my old clothes for gently used ones at the consignment shop downtown. I haven't spent a dime. And for your information, I've already cut up all the credit cards."

"I'm sorry." In three long strides he stood in front of her chair. Their gazes locked. "But, Lynn, you don't have to dress…differently. I gave my word. I won't force myself on you again."

Her cheeks burned, and she looked at the door, longing for escape. Start as you mean to go on. Face the issue and move past it. No more doormat. She stiffened her spine and held her ground. "Sawyer, you didn't force me. We both got a little crazy and lost control. We were hurting and needed comfort."

The muscle along his jaw twitched. "A woman doesn't go from calendar girl to corporate career woman overnight without a damn good reason."

Calendar girl? Her? She nearly laughed out loud. Did that mean he found her attractive? Her breath caught. "For your information, I'm dressing this way because I want to, not because of…not because of what happened between us."

His disbelieving gaze traveled over her again. "You're certain that this makeover has nothing to do with the intimacy between us?"

She wet her suddenly dry lips and tired to ignore the sizzle in her veins. "Yes."

His eyes narrowed. "Brett's only been gone three weeks. You're making a lot of drastic changes that you're going to regret later."

"I don't think I'll have regrets."

Shoving his hands in his pockets, he leaned against the polished desktop and crossed his ankles. His pant leg brushed against her shin. Her pulse jumped erratically. She didn't think he intentionally crowded her. Sawyer just took up so much…space in the room, in her mind, in her dreams. Inside her body. *Stop it, Lynn. Don't think about it.* Her skin prickled, and warmth gathered between her thighs. She shifted her legs to the side and leaned back in the chair.

He twisted to reach for something on his desk. The fabric of his trousers stretched to outline thickly muscled thighs and his maleness.

She quickly averted her eyes, but heat scorched her cheeks and a few other places. The memory of his taut muscles flexing between her legs and the tickle of his wiry hairs against the sensitive skin of her inner thighs made her stomach flutter and her lower abdomen ache. She bit her lip and pressed her knees together. It was one thing to still dream about that night under the cover of darkness, but she shouldn't have thoughts like that here in the office in broad daylight. Before she could tamp down her body's unexpected and unwelcome tightening, he faced her again.

His gaze met and searched hers. She thought she saw a corresponding fire ignite in his blue eyes, but then he blinked, frowned and directed his attention to the file folder containing her flyer material.

"Lynn, this is good." His voice had a rough edge. "I've made a few suggestions. Incorporate those and then save the file on a disk, and we'll drop it by the printer's this afternoon."

She braced herself, waiting for the *but* for a full thirty seconds. It didn't come. She'd expected Sawyer to point out her faults—the way Brett always had. "You liked it?"

"Yes. You hit every point I wanted to emphasize." His praise exhilarated her. "Brett couldn't have done a better job."

A wave of guilt blindsided her. She took the file from him and dipped her chin. Her husband was the last person she thought of when Sawyer looked at her with approval in his eyes. She scanned the pages and then stared at him in surprise. "It will take me less than five minutes to make these changes."

"Like I said, it's good." He folded his arms and appraised her for several tense, silent seconds. She squirmed in her chair. "Care to explain how you knew what to put into a promo flyer?"

"Not really."

His jaw set. "Wrong answer."

Brett would have laughed himself into a hernia if he'd ever found out, but Sawyer's direct gaze made her feel like an insect pinned to an entomologist's board. She suspected he wouldn't let her leave until she gave him the information he wanted. "Brett kept all of his old college textbooks in the attic. I read them."

His brows lowered and his lips thinned. "You read the texts and learned this on your own?"

His carefully neutral tone made her clench her teeth. Was he setting her up only to cut her down? She lifted her chin. "Yes."

He muttered what sounded like a curse under his breath, straightened and circled around behind his desk, stopping on the opposite side. He leaned forward, bracing himself on straight arms. The hair on the back of her neck rose at the anger burning in his eyes. "He said you flunked out. That you…weren't cut out to be a student."

Brett had certainly told her often enough that he didn't think she was smart enough to attend college. *I don't want to waste my money,* he'd said, and he'd probably reported as much to his brother. "I didn't have time to study, and my grades weren't good, but I didn't fail."

"Then why did you quit?"

Her husband had resented the time she spent studying and every moment she spent outside the house, but she wouldn't tell him that. "Brett believed that my studies were interfering with our marriage."

He narrowed his eyes and a muscle twitched in his jaw. "He made you quit?"

She didn't want to tarnish his image of his baby brother. "The final decision was mine."

He snorted in disbelief. "Once we're married, you can go back to school. You don't have to work."

A lump formed in her throat, and her neck muscles knotted. Oh, how she wished she could take him up on that offer, but she'd been down that road before and learned a few hard lessons. Once Brett started working for Sawyer, she'd quit her job to attend college the way they'd planned. Not only had she become almost a prisoner in her own home, she'd given Brett the right to demand she justify every penny of his money that she'd spent. That his brother might try to hem her in the same way made her skin feel two sizes too tight. No matter how much she yearned to get an education she refused to repeat that error.

She closed the folder with a snap. "I want to work."

"It's not necessary."

"For me, it is."

His brows dipped. "Lynn—"

"Sawyer, I never planned to be unemployed. Except for the years I was married, I've worked since I was fourteen years old." Her father had been a firm believer in the Idle Hands Make Mischief theory. Sawyer's eyes narrowed, and she rushed on before he could object. "I want to work until the baby comes. Afterward, I'd still like to work at least part-time. If you don't want me here, I'll find a job elsewhere."

His fists clenched and his jaw muscles bunched. "My not wanting you here is not an issue. You used to dream of going to college. I thought you'd want to stay home with the baby or go back to school. You can do both. We'll hire someone to watch the baby while you're in class."

What he proposed sounded too good to be true—like Brett's offer had years ago, but her rose-colored glasses were gone, and she wasn't stupid enough to get her hopes up again. Some lessons you didn't need to learn twice. "I do, but—"

"Think about it. We have plenty of time to make those decisions." He pulled his date book forward, effectively ending the discussion. "Once you've made the changes to the brochure, we'll go to the courthouse to apply for the marriage license. We have an appointment to be married Wednesday afternoon at three o'clock. If you'd like to invite any guests, feel free.''

The butterflies in her stomach turned into 747s. He was moving too fast. Her head spun. ''I don't have anyone except my aunt, and she's not well enough to travel.''

He closed his date book with a snap. ''Okay. Your rooms are finished. You can start moving your stuff in this evening.''

She swallowed hard, trying to subdue her rising panic. ''This is kind of sudden, isn't it?''

''Why wait?'' He dug in his pocket and offered her a key. ''Here's a key to my house.''

When she hesitated, he caught her hand, pressed the key into her palm and closed her fingers around it. The metal had absorbed his body heat, and the hand enclosing hers was every bit as hot as she remembered. Her muscles locked. Before she could come up with a logical reason to refuse the key, Opal tapped on the door and then stuck her head inside the gap. ''Ms. Riggan, your real estate agent is on the phone.''

Sawyer released her and motioned for her to take his seat behind the desk. He moved to stand beside the window. ''Put him through, please, Opal. Lynn will take the call in here.''

Lynn's knees shook so badly she could barely stand and walk around Sawyer's desk. She sank into his high-backed leather chair. Unlike Brett's stiff seat, this chair had been broken in. It cradled her in soft, supple leather. Sawyer's spicy scent surrounded her. Her mind tumbled back to the night on the stairs and the way he'd smelled when she'd buried her face in his neck.

Her heart hammered triple time and her palms grew

damp. How could just thinking about Sawyer have this effect on her when actually being with her husband never had?

The light on the phone blinked, drawing her from her unwelcome thoughts. She lifted the receiver and listened to the agent with numb acceptance. They'd had an excellent cash offer on the house. Could she be out by the end of the month?

Panic swelled inside her. Doubts tumbled through her mind. Everything inside her screamed *No,* but with foreclosure and Brett's debts hanging over her head she had no choice. She said yes.

Hanging up the phone, she parked her elbows on Sawyer's desk and dropped her head into her hands. Like it or not, she'd committed to marrying Sawyer and to moving into his home.

Dear God, please don't let this be another mistake.

Five

Sawyer would be here any minute, and Lynn wasn't ready—but then, she'd probably never be ready to get married again. The thought saddened her, since a large family was the one thing she wanted most.

She set her hairbrush down on the bathroom counter and pressed a hand below her navel. This child would be her family. No, it wouldn't be the number of children she'd once yearned for, but it would be enough. It would have to be.

Yanking the wedding ring Brett had given her from her finger, she threaded a thin gold chain through the plain band. Her hands trembled so much that she could barely fasten the catch behind her neck. The necklace would be a talisman to remind her that this would be a short-term marriage of convenience, a business deal lasting only until Sawyer could buy her share of the company. Love had nothing to do with it. She dropped the ring into the scooped neck of her dress.

She'd spent hours with Brett's journal last night, rereading his cryptic notes and trying to find a way out of this wedding. Brett had mentioned money he'd made, but she'd found no trace of it in their accounts. And then his derogatory comments about her had made her sick to her stomach, and she'd put the journal aside.

How could she not have known he never loved her? And why, then, had he married her? How had he fooled her so completely? And what did he mean by, "As long as he held what Sawyer valued most he held the upper hand?" She'd have to go back to the journal, not a prospect she relished, but there was something in it that she couldn't quite figure out. Some of the comments seemed to be written in some code or something.

The doorbell rang and her stomach lurched. She clenched the countertop until the nausea passed and then slowly made her way downstairs.

She opened the door to find Sawyer on her welcome mat. Her pulse jumped. He looked devastatingly handsome in his black suit, blinding-white shirt and pewter tie. He'd pinned a single ivory rosebud with a sprig of baby's breath to his lapel. His jaw gleamed from an afternoon shave, and his hair had been freshly trimmed. Any outsider would believe him to be an attentive groom.

His cobalt gaze slid over her slowly, thoroughly, and her skin tingled in its wake. "Where's the Mercedes? Whose car is in your garage?"

She swallowed to ease the dryness in her mouth. "I traded the Mercedes in last night for something more practical."

His brows dipped. "Brett gave you that car for your twenty-first birthday."

"Yes, he did, but I'd prefer to drive something I don't have to make payments on." If she hadn't traded it in, the bank would have repossessed it. She'd been lucky to find a decent used car for the amount of equity she had in the convertible.

His lips thinned. "You loved that car."

Yes she had. The sports car was everything she wasn't: fun, sporty, classy and sexy. But she wasn't up for a debate over her debt-ridden vehicle when she had a wedding to worry about. Her nerves were rattled and her mind in turmoil. "Sawyer, it's just a car, and the sedan is much more practical for carrying a car seat."

He acknowledged her point with brisk nod. "Are you ready?"

"As ready as I'll ever be."

The softening of his expression warmed her. "Lynn, we'll make this work."

She wished she believed him, and as Tina Turner sang, "What's love got to do with it?"

"Let's go."

She grabbed her purse from the hall table and followed him out into the summer heat. Ten minutes later her heart skipped a beat when he parked in front of the historic stone church. Her mouth dried and her stomach knotted. She'd expected a quick, anonymous civil service like her last marriage.

The fabric of her pale-peach sundress clung to her suddenly damp skin, and the matching lace jacket chafed her neck. She plucked at the collar and fingered her necklace.

Sawyer circled the front of the vehicle, opened her door and extended his hand. Her muscles went rigid.

She wasn't sure she could force herself to walk up the sun-dappled, cobblestone path to the arched and elaborately carved front doors. His shuttered gaze held hers. With her nerves quivering like harp strings, she placed her palm over his. The warmth of his grasp enclosed her cold fingers as he gently tugged her from the SUV and shut the door.

Her knees knocked. She concentrated on conquering the telling motion. Her mouth dried. Sawyer opened the back passenger door and then closed it again, but she didn't look to see why. She focused on the steeple, the future and all the reasons she'd agreed to this farce. Security for her child. A roof over her head. Enough money to get an education and start over. Sawyer's touch on her arm startled her.

"These are for you." He offered her a bouquet of cream-colored roses intertwined with ivy and baby's breath.

Brett never bought flowers unless guilt was involved, but no guilty secrets lurked in Sawyer's direct gaze. The unexpected and thoughtful gesture brought tears to her eyes. She hid her emotional reaction by inhaling the heady scent. "You shouldn't have."

He shrugged. "I wanted to, and I guessed from all the roses in your yard that you like them."

"They're my favorite flower."

Two vehicles pulled into the lot and parked. Opal climbed from the closest car and a broad-shouldered, dark-haired man Lynn had never met climbed from the other.

Sawyer transferred his hand to her waist and guided her toward the flagstone sidewalk. The heat of his touch penetrated the thin linen of her dress, and her stomach muscles clenched. "Lynn, this is Carter Jones, my college roommate. Opal and Carter will be our witnesses."

She tried to think of something polite to say, but her brain refused to stumble past the fact that she was standing outside of a church with marriage on her mind. She shook Carter's hand and managed to croak out, "Hello."

He nodded briskly. The coolness in his steely eyes was as hard to miss as the disapproving set of his mouth.

"Shall we?" Sawyer swept a hand toward the church.

Her legs moved forward in jerky, disjointed steps. Sawyer had bent over backward for Brett, and he'd do the same for the child she carried. She thumbed her bare ring finger and then touched the necklace thumping against her breastbone. For her sake—*for her baby's sake*—she needed to be strong.

The inside of the church was cool and dark after the hot and humid June afternoon. The dramatic change in temperature made her grateful for her lace jacket, but she shivered nonetheless. Colored light filtered through the stained glass windows, painting the candlelit front of the church in Monet colors. The preacher waited there.

Lynn's first instinct was to run. One loveless marriage had been enough to last a lifetime, but her first marriage had begun with love—at least on her part. This one lacked even that illusion. Maybe that was a good thing. They both knew where they stood. Hearts wouldn't be broken.

Sawyer introduced the preacher and the two men quietly discussed the formalities while Lynn waited and tried to still the shaking of her bouquet.

Opal touched her sleeve. ''You look lovely. Doesn't she, Sawyer?''

Lynn's heart flip-flopped. Her gaze met Sawyer's and a spark ignited in her midsection at his thorough head-to-toe inspection. She thought she saw a corresponding flicker in his eyes, but then he blinked and it was gone. ''Stunning.''

Her breath caught. ''Th-thank you.''

The preacher beamed. ''Are we ready?''

No! Lynn swallowed the lump in her throat and forced a smile. ''Yes.''

''Do you have the rings?''

Her heart nearly tumbled from her chest when Sawyer withdrew his parents' beautifully engraved wedding bands from his pocket and laid them on the preacher's open Bible.

Her throat closed up and tears stung her eyes. Her sham of a marriage would be sealed with a Riggan family heirloom.

She felt like a fraud.

The service was brief and to the point. Sawyer clasped Lynn's cold hand in his and eased the gold band over her knuckle and into the groove left by his brother's ring.

The preacher instructed him to kiss his bride. Lynn's face turned a delicate pink and she dampened her lips. Sawyer's mouth dried. He wasn't supposed to desire her, but today she looked more like the woman he'd wanted years ago and less like the flashy woman he'd known as Brett's wife. Her summery dress floated over her slim curves with a subtle sexiness that revved his heart into a higher gear, and her hair draped over her shoulders like champagne-colored satin.

Damn, he wished she'd kept the sex-kitten wardrobe. Her sexy, seductive clothing had reminded him that she belonged to Brett and made it easier to resist her.

His chest constricted at the dampness in her eyes. She still grieved for his brother, and he'd railroaded her into marriage. Short of a court order, he hadn't had a choice if he wanted to keep her from fleeing to Florida and carrying her baby with her.

Sawyer cupped her elbows and leaned forward to touch his mouth to hers. Her sweet honeysuckle scent wrapped around him, and instead of one brief kiss, his lips lingered on the softness of hers until her cool flesh warmed and became pliant under his. The urge to pull her close and plunder her mouth raced through his blood like a forest fire, nearly consuming him. It took all he had to muster the strength to release her. He studied her flushed cheeks and damp lips, and his groin tightened.

How could she kiss him like that if she still loved Brett? Or was she thinking of his brother when she closed her eyes? Acid burned his stomach, and his suit coat felt too tight. He shifted his shoulders.

In the anteroom Sawyer signed the document the preacher put in front of him, and Lynn signed her name beside his—the same name she'd signed after marrying Brett. The burn in Sawyer's gut increased. He'd married his brother's wife, become his brother's temporary replacement. After so many years of thinking of Lynn as taboo, she suddenly wasn't, in a legal sense, but she hadn't married *him* out of love and, like her name, their relationship wasn't going to change.

Outside, while Opal fussed over Lynn's bouquet, Sawyer followed Carter to his car. Throughout the service he'd felt Carter's disapproval. His best friend and his brother had never gotten along, and Carter had been vocal in his arguments against this marriage when Sawyer had called to ask him to be his best man. Given Carter's objections, his willingness to stand beside him today meant a hell of a lot.

"Thanks." Sawyer offered his hand.

After a brief hesitation, Carter grasped it. "I hope you know what you're getting yourself into."

"Brett would have wanted me to look out for Lynn."

Carter snorted. "Brett only wanted you to want her. Look, man, you know I love you like a brother, but you have a blind spot where Brett's concerned. Keep your eyes on Lynn. She might have an ulterior motive for agreeing to this marriage."

"She's pregnant." Sawyer ground his teeth at Carter's I-told-you-so expression. He didn't dare reveal the whole truth—not even to his best friend.

"You can count on me…no matter what." Carter climbed into his Mustang and drove off in a spray of gravel.

Sawyer returned to the women and was struck anew by the fact that Lynn was now his wife. *His* wife. His beautiful, sexy-as-hell wife. And he couldn't touch her except in a platonic way. Adrenaline raced through his bloodstream, making his heart pound and his chest tighten. Get over it, Riggan.

He placed his hand on her waist and faced Opal. "You know how to reach me. Lynn and I will see you on Monday."

Lynn's spine stiffened beneath his fingertips. Her wide blue eyes stared up at him with a touch of panic in their depths, and her teeth dug into her bottom lip. He hadn't clued her in on their so-called honeymoon plans. She swallowed, drawing his attention to the wildly fluttering pulse in her throat. The memory of pressing his mouth there while he'd been buried deep inside her blindsided him. He barely heard Opal promising to limit her calls to emergencies before she left.

He escorted Lynn to his vehicle, returned her bouquet to the box in the back seat and then leaned in once she'd climbed inside. The sun bounced off his father's wedding band with a blinding light as he reached for her seat belt, and his mother's ring glistened on Lynn's finger when she reached at the same time. His hand met hers over the buckle.

"I can get it." She shook his hand off and clicked metal to metal. "Why are we taking the rest of the week off?"

He shoved his hands in his pockets and studied the top of her head when she didn't look at him. "Because it'll give us the time to get you settled in my house."

She closed her eyes briefly and then lifted her gaze. "I wish you'd warned me."

What was the problem? She'd avoided moving any of her belongings into his house, even though her rooms had been finished for days. He wanted the job done. He wanted Lynn in his home. He couldn't explain the sudden surge of protectiveness and possessiveness welling up inside him. "Isn't the estate agent coming to pick up the rest of your furniture tomorrow?"

"Yes, he says he can get a better price if he takes everything back to his showroom to display and sell."

He shrugged. "Now you have time off to supervise him."

Her fingers knotted in her lap. "But I haven't earned any paid vacation days yet. It was bad enough that I had to take half a day off today. Can we stop by the office so I can pick up some work? I can read over the intern applications at home. Otherwise, I'll have more time to make up."

He didn't know what kind of objections he expected, but Lynn not wanting time off wasn't even remotely close. Brett had never called her lazy or stupid, but he'd implied it when he said she was a great wife as long as he kept her in her place—the kitchen or the bedroom. Sawyer shifted uncomfortably at the thought of Lynn in Brett's bed.

"You're on salary. It's not an issue." It had been an issue with his brother, who'd missed as many days as possible. Picking up his slack had become part of Sawyer's and Opal's regular workload, but Brett was a marketing genius so Sawyer had overlooked his slack work ethic.

Lynn looked ready to argue. He held up his hand. "Carter and a couple of other guys are meeting us at your place in an hour. We'll move the bulk of your belongings to my house tonight."

He wished he could erase the cornered look from her eyes. "I'm sure Carter's thrilled about that."

He sighed, regretting that Lynn had picked up on the undercurrents. "Give him time. He'll come around."

She didn't look convinced. "Does he know this is a temporary marriage?"

"No, and I'm not offering explanations to anyone. It's none of their business."

She sighed, laid her head back on the headrest and closed her eyes. She looked tired. He fisted his hand on the urge to trace the lavender circles beneath the fan of her eyelashes.

"Don't worry about anything except keeping you and your baby healthy."

"And the company."

He ground his teeth on the reminder that Lynn had agreed to this marriage for monetary reasons. ''Right. But the company's health is my problem.''

Her lids lifted and the wariness she'd worn since that night in her foyer was back. ''I don't have much to move. I'm only keeping the furniture in my—the guest bedroom, my clothes and the boxes of household stuff that I couldn't sell.''

''Then tonight you'll sleep in your own bed in my house. There's plenty of room for the rest in my garage.'' The thought of Lynn sleeping down the hall made him feel restless. He loosened the knot of his tie. Moments ago he'd stood in church and promised to love, honor and cherish her for the rest of his days.

Would the lie send him straight to hell or would the next twelve months just feel like it?

Ill at ease, Lynn stood on the fringe of the big farmhouse kitchen. She was used to RSVPs and formal parties, the kind of stilted affair her husband had preferred.

The boisterous group of four men and three women circled around Sawyer's kitchen island and dove into the pizzas as soon as the delivery man left. They settled at the table or on bar stools at the island, ate off paper plates and drank their sodas or beers straight from the can. They didn't expect Lynn to wait on them or to clean up after them. They expected her to pull up a chair and join them. After years of isolation, it was a bit intimidating...even without Carter's constant scowling.

''Lynn, you need to eat.'' Sawyer's quiet voice in her ear startled her out of her introspection.

After the ceremony he'd changed into a gray sleeveless T-shirt and a pair of cutoff denim shorts. She hadn't been able to take her eyes off him as he loaded her meager belongings into his friends' trucks. The bunching and flexing of his muscles had reminded her of his strength the night he'd held her and—

She interrupted the forbidden thought, looked away from his bulging biceps and wiped her palms on her slacks. Sawyer wrapped a big hand around her upper arm and tugged her across the tile floor toward the table. The warmth of his touch remained even after he set a plate of pizza and a can of her favorite soda in front of her and returned to the bar to retrieve his own dinner.

Brett had been a charmer, but he never could have picked up the phone and had friends with pickup trucks cheerfully agree to move furniture. Sawyer's friends had brought girlfriends, and in two short hours this crew had packed and loaded her belongings into their vehicles, driven here and unloaded. They asked for nothing in return.

She kept waiting for the catch.

The men had installed her brass bed upstairs in Sawyer's renovated guest suite. The women had complimented her on decorating the suite so beautifully, but she wasn't the one responsible for the soft-buttery-yellow walls or the Dresden-blue wood trim. Sawyer had chosen the paints to complement the hand-stitched quilt she kept on her bed. Why would he be so thoughtful? She couldn't help but be leery of his generosity. Brett's good deeds had always come with strings attached.

"Where's Maggie?" one of the women asked.

Maggie? Had Sawyer been involved with someone when he'd suggested this marriage agreement? Brett had often remarked on the parade of women through Sawyer's life, and he'd often speculated on just why

Sawyer couldn't stick with one woman more than a few months. A chill washed over Lynn. Would she have a second husband who cheated on her? Sawyer had said he wouldn't. Not that it mattered, since this wasn't a love match, but she would prefer not to be humiliated.

"I put her in the laundry room while we had the doors propped open. Mind if I let her out?"

"No," the group answered as one.

"Lynn?" Sawyer's hand cupped her shoulder and his warmth seeped into her skin.

Okay, so Maggie wasn't a woman. "Who or what's Maggie?"

"My neighbor's dog. Rick found her on a job site and brought her home, but he's working out of town for a few weeks, and he asked me to keep an eye on her. Mind if I let her out?" he repeated.

"No, I love dogs." She'd wanted one for years, but dogs soiled expensive, white-carpeted houses and immaculately landscaped backyards, so a dog had been out of the question.

Sawyer crossed the kitchen to open the door. A long-haired rust-colored, mostly Irish setter waddled out, crossed the room and settled on a rug by the door. Lynn's mouth fell open. "She's pregnant."

Sawyer grimaced. "Very. And if Rick doesn't come home soon I'm going to be a father instead of an uncle."

The others laughed and teased him, but Lynn's gaze held Sawyer's and her breath caught. The similarity between her life and the dog situation was too obvious to miss. Would Sawyer be a father or an uncle? Did he want her baby to be his? The possibility of spending the rest of her life tangled in this sexual tug-of-war each time her child had visitations with Sawyer made her shiver.

Sawyer pulled a barstool up to the table and set his plate beside Lynn's. He looked at her untouched food. "Would you rather have something else?"

The concern darkening his eyes pulled at something inside her. She wanted to believe—oh, how she wanted to believe—in the picture of domestic bliss he painted, even if it was only temporary.

"No, this is really good." She wasn't referring to the pizza which she'd yet to taste. Years ago, when she'd imagined married life, this loud and friendly get-together with a big, old house and a dog was exactly what she'd pictured. Her fantasies bore absolutely no resemblance to her marriage—she gulped—her *first* marriage. The ring currently on her finger signified a new start—one that she'd never anticipated and didn't know how to handle. This new relationship scared her, because Sawyer made her feel things that Brett never had, and he made her hope. She'd learned the hard way that hopes led to disappointments.

Her stomach grumbled, making her aware that she was indeed hungry for the first time in months. She bit into the gooey cheese and listened to the good-natured teasing going on around her. Laughter bounced off the high, beamed ceiling and the tile floor. She could almost imagine the noisy, happy sounds of children playing in the room while their mother rolled sugar cookies on the long kitchen island. Sawyer had installed all new appliances, so cooking for a family would be a joy—a joy she would never experience.

It seemed a little odd that, with the exception of Carter, Sawyer's friends had accepted her into their midst without question, despite the fact that less than a month ago she'd been married to his brother. For the first time in her adult life Lynn felt as if she belonged, and she had Sawyer to thank for that. He'd taken her into his home and drawn her into his circle of friends.

He laughed at one of Carter's remarks. The sound rippled down Lynn's spine. He shifted and his thigh and shoulder brushed hers. Her breath caught. He treated her as if she were the woman he loved and not just an obligation he'd assumed.

This was what marriage was supposed to be.

Too bad it was a sham, and a temporary one at that.

Alone on their wedding night.

The door closed behind the last of their guests, and a deafening silence descended over the house. Lynn shifted on her feet in the front hall under Sawyer's watchful gaze. Her heart pounded hard in her chest. Time to find out if his kindness came with strings. She wiped her damp palms on her slacks. "Your friends are nice."

"Yeah. They liked you too, but—" Sawyer snapped his jaw closed and turned away.

She braced herself. After each of their rare social engagements Brett had engaged in a postmortem of her faux pas. An uncomfortable prickle crawled up her neck, and she dug her nails into her palms. She wanted to get this over with. "But what?"

He sighed before facing her. "You overdid it."

Did he mean she'd laughed too often? Talked too much? Or that she looked like a hag? She studied her reflection in the antique mirror hanging in Sawyer's foyer and grimaced. The khaki slacks and pale-pink blouse she'd changed into after the wedding were wrinkled and soiled. Her makeup had faded and wisps of her hair had escaped the barrette restraining it to hang around her face and neck, but it had been a long and emotional day. Would he fault her for looking a little ragged?

He stepped closer until her shoulder brushed the middle of his chest and the mirror framed them both. The warmth of his body reached hers, spreading down the length of her arm as effectively as a caress. Her pulse leaped and her mouth dried. Her skin suddenly seemed more sensitive to the weight of her clothing and the whisper of his breath on her temple.

A frown puckered his brows. He lifted his hand, hesitated and then tucked a lock of hair behind her ear. Goose bumps raced over her skin. "I shouldn't have let you do so much."

His softly spoken words made her jerk up her chin and squint at him in surprise. She'd expected condemnation and instead she got...*concern?* "Are you kidding? Every time I lifted something bigger than a shoebox one of your friends took it away from me." And then realization dawned. "They know, don't they?"

He didn't blink. "Yeah."

She closed her eyes, swallowed and then lifted her lids again. "What did you tell them?"

"That you're expecting."

She pressed her cold hands to her hot cheeks. "What must they think of me? Either they'll believe I've shackled one man to be a father to his brother's baby or that I've cheated on my husband."

Irritation flashed in his eyes, but his gaze held hers and his hand settled low on her belly. Warmth spread from his palm outward, and she could feel the imprint of each long finger. "My friends are not the kind to make judgments, and even if they were, I don't care what anyone else thinks. I will be a father to this child. I'll be there when he or she is born and for every Little League game or ballet recital thereafter. God willing, I'll be there for graduations, a wedding and the day I become a grandfather.''

Her throat closed up. She couldn't breathe. She ought to be alarmed by the possessive tone of his voice, but he painted the picture she'd yearned for most of her life, what she craved for her baby. Her parents hadn't been there to see her graduate from high school or for her weddings. Neither her parents nor Sawyer's would be around to cradle their first grandchild. Tears stung her eyes, and she blinked furiously to banish them. Tears were a sign of weakness, and each time she'd cried in front of Brett, he'd gone for the jugular.

''Shhh. Don't.'' Sawyer turned her into his arms, cupped his hand over her hair and pressed her face to his shoulder. His heart beat steadily beneath her cheek. She hiccuped with the effort to hold back the sob his unexpected tenderness evoked and fought the urge to burrow into him and absorb his strength. His scent wrapped around her and his kindness softened her bitter heart. Yet she heard a warning in her head—don't get your hopes up.

He lifted her chin with a fingertip and swept her tears away with his thumbs. ''I didn't mean to make you cry.''

With his head tipped toward hers, his mouth hovered just inches away. His breath swept her face, making her yearn to rise on her tiptoes, press her lips to his and find the oblivion he'd given her that night. She wet her lips, and his eyes traced the movement. Heat flickered in his eyes, and the fine hairs on her body rose. Her fingers flexed in anticipation of stroking the five-o'clock shadow on his jaw. He leaned closer.

Maggie squeezed between them, whimpering to go out. Shocked by her behavior, Lynn took a hasty step back. She petted the dog and silently thanked her for the interruption. Kissing Sawyer would have been a colossal mistake. Relinquishing control always brought consequences. She'd been down this road before and could be carrying Sawyer's child as a result. Sucking in a sharp breath, she straightened her spine.

Sawyer shoved a hand through his hair and grabbed Maggie's leash off the credenza.

She eyed his rigid shoulders suspiciously. Was he angry that she'd rebuffed him? Had his gentleness been an attempt to soften her up to get her into bed? That was the kind of thing Brett would have done. Hadn't she learned that men could separate lust and love?

The difference was that Sawyer roused her emotions. He made her feel needy and hungry and cherished in a way his brother never had. She wanted to make love with him again, to feel that heady rush of feminine power, but she wouldn't because she could easily see herself falling for him if he kept up this subtle attack on her senses. Getting her heart involved would be a huge mistake. They were roommates, nothing more.

He attached the leash to Maggie's collar and faced her. The tension deepening the laugh lines on his face didn't look like anger. "Lynn, this is your home now. If you need anything, help yourself. I'm going to take Maggie for a walk. Good night."

He led the dog out the front door and shut it behind him with a controlled click. Very unlike his brother.

Lynn stared after him. What did he want from her? He had to want something. Other than the baby she carried, she couldn't think of anything Sawyer stood to gain from this relationship.

Before she could figure it out, the cumulative effects of the day hit her, weighing her limbs with exhaustion and muddling her thinking. She dragged herself up the sweeping semicircular staircase and went to bed alone on her wedding night.

An emotionless, temporary marriage was exactly what she wanted. Why did she feel so empty and alone?

Six

Sawyer's coffee mug slipped from his grasp and crashed on the tile floor. He swore, and Maggie scrambled under the kitchen table. Had having Lynn in his house turned him into a klutz?

Discounting his mother and the dog, he'd never lived with a female before. Not even his former fiancée had wanted to set up house, and that was a good thing, since Pam had broken their engagement the minute he'd stated his intention to file for custody of his sixteen-year-old brother.

Sawyer grabbed the dustpan and broom and swept up the shattered mess. Lynn's bedroom door creaked, signaling that he'd woken her. Damn. Her steps raced down the stairs. She skidded to a halt inside the doorway as he emptied the dustpan into the trash.

His breath lodged in his throat. With her flushed face and short, silky, leg-baring robe, she looked sexy.

Damned sexy. Desire slammed him with the force of a Mack truck.

Wide-eyed, she shoved back her tangled, rumpled hair with one hand and clutched the lapels of her robe together with the other. "I'm sorry. I overslept. If you'll give me a couple of minutes I'll have breakfast ready in no time. Tell me what time you'd like to eat tomorrow. I promise I'll have it waiting when you come downstairs."

He frowned at her rushed words and nervous tone. "I don't expect you to cook my breakfast."

Her brows dipped. She eyed him cautiously. "You don't?"

"I can feed myself." He tapped the box of Frosted Flakes sitting on the counter.

The wariness left her by slow increments, easing the tight set of her mouth and shoulders and relaxing the stiffness of her spine. She blinked and then her gaze glided over his bare chest to the waistband of his gym shorts—which he'd pulled on only because she was in the house—and down his legs. His blood raced in the same direction as if she'd stroked him with her hands. His body jerked to life under her perusal—something his thin shorts couldn't hide.

Color flooded her cheeks. She took a hit-and-run glance at his face from beneath her gold-tipped lashes and then turned her head, hugging her arms around herself. "I heard a crash."

"Dropped my mug. Sorry I woke you." His voice came out gravelly. He cleared his throat. He hadn't intended to embarrass her or himself, but his body reacted like a compass to the North Pole whenever she was near. He hadn't had this problem before that night in her foyer, but now that he knew how she tasted and how the hot clench of her internal muscles would surround him, his control had crashed like a virus-infected hard drive.

"I should be up already. You didn't cut yourself?" He caught another brief glimpse of her blue eyes before she ducked her chin and busied herself with tying the belt of her robe.

"No. We aren't going into the office today, so you can take it easy. Lie by the pool or put your feet up until it's time to meet the estate appraiser."

"Is that what you're going to do?" She lifted a hand to smooth her hair, and her robe slipped off the opposite shoulder, revealing the spaghetti-thin strap of whatever she wore underneath the slippery fabric.

Oh man, he did not need to think about what she wore—or wasn't wearing—beneath that robe. He couldn't swallow, couldn't breathe. Gritting his teeth, he pinched the slick material and dragged it back up to cover her creamy skin. Damn his overactive libido. Clenching his fist, he retreated to the toaster before she noticed just how strongly she'd affected him.

She'd asked a question. He glanced back over his shoulder but kept his hips facing the counter. "I'm going to stain the wainscoting in the dining room this morning."

She nibbled her lip and shifted on her long, bare legs. "Would you like some help for a couple of hours?"

An extra set of hands would make the job go faster, but only if he could keep his mind on his work. "Your choice. The stain's nontoxic, and the room's well ventilated. If you can stand the smell, I wouldn't refuse the help. This is a big house and it's taking me a long time to restore it one room at a time."

"Then count me in. If I'm going to live here, then the least I can do is help with your renovations. You've done a beautiful job so far."

"Thanks. Breakfast first?"

She looked tempted. "I should get dressed and put on my makeup before inflicting myself on you. I only came down because I thought you might be hurt."

He'd have to get used to someone worrying about him again. Other than Opal's occasional motherly advice, nobody had in ten years. And then her words sank in. *Inflicting herself on him?* What did she mean by that? Her averted face gave no clues.

"Lynn, this is your home, not a hotel. You don't have to get dressed or paint your face before you leave your room. Hell, you can walk around in your pajamas all day if you want." He hoped she didn't. He was all too aware that there were only a couple of layers of silk between him and bare skin. Would the rest of her skin be the same creamy shade as her upper thighs?

Get your brain out of your shorts, Riggan. "Eat something before you get sick. Toast?"

Maggie ambled over and pressed her snout into Lynn's hand. Lynn knelt to pet the dog, and her robe rode up to the top of her thighs. Sawyer nearly swallowed his tongue. He could practically feel her smooth skin against his palms. He bit back a groan. However long it took him to raise the money to buy her out was going to be too long.

"Okay." Lynn looked longingly at the coffeepot. "I'm going to miss coffee."

"We'll switch to decaf," he choked out and shoved two slices of bread in the toaster with more force than necessary.

"I probably should avoid caffeine, but I was thinking more along the lines of coffee isn't going to agree with me for a while."

He jerked his gaze back to her face. Now that she mentioned it, her color had faded, and she looked a little green. He didn't want her to be sick. Weird thought. Pregnant women got sick all the time, but for some reason it bothered him to see Lynn suffer. He grabbed a glass out of the cabinet and set it on the counter in front of her. "Juice and milk are in the fridge. Help yourself."

She hovered indecisively. The toast popped up. He dropped the slices onto a plate, set them on the breakfast bar and nudged the dish toward her. He turned back to add more bread to the toaster. The pang he felt over losing his brother battled with a jealous burn in his belly. Brett had shared four years' worth of breakfasts with Lynn—years of seeing her sleepy, mussed and sexy first thing in the morning. Or had she always come downstairs dressed and made up for the day? If so, then why? She didn't strike him as the vain type of woman who never strayed far from a mirror. He ought to know. He'd dated his share of those.

He took a bracing swig of coffee before facing her. "If you don't want strawberry there're other kinds of jelly in the fridge. I have cereal and there are some eggs on the top shelf."

"Toast is fine." She washed her hands and then opened the refrigerator. The teasing twinkle in the smile she flashed over her shoulder slammed the breath right out of him. "You have a sweet tooth. The cereal was a hint, but your jelly collection is a dead giveaway."

He poked the knife clear through his bread, and the

cold strawberry preserves blobbed on his palm. ''Yeah, and I maintain a gym membership to support my bad habit.''

She laughed and the sound stopped him in his tracks. He'd forgotten Lynn's laugh. Sure, she'd chuckled a couple of times over pizza last night, but that wasn't the same as her throaty, full-bodied, sexy-as-hell laugh. The sound reminded him of those nights four and a half years ago when he'd walked her home after work and stolen kisses in the shadows where the moonlight and streetlights didn't penetrate. He gulped more coffee and scalded his tongue.

She poured herself a glass of orange juice and slathered a thick layer of grape jelly onto her bread. He gestured to her breakfast. ''Looks like I'm not the only one with a sweet tooth.''

The corners of her mouth, dotted with purple jelly, turned up. The urge to lick that sticky substance from her, to taste the heat and the passion of her mouth, made his heart pound. He moistened his dry lips, pulled in a slow breath and lifted his gaze to hers.

Her smile faded, and awareness arched between them. Her nipples peaked beneath the thin robe, and her breasts rose and fell on a slow breath. She broke the connection by reaching for a paper napkin and wiping her mouth.

He clenched his hand around his mug, shifted to relieve the pressure in his groin and prayed for strength to ignore the attraction between them. He'd had his chance with Lynn years ago, and she'd made her choice when she ignored his letter and married his brother.

But, damn, he wanted his wife in the worst kind of way.

* * *

''Stop. Back up.'' Sawyer's command halted Lynn at the threshold of the dining room. ''You can't wear that to paint.''

She looked down at her coordinated exercise outfit. Brett had insisted she always look presentable—even when cleaning the house or sweating to one of the two dozen exercise videos he'd bought her. The lavender shorts and shirt were the most casual clothes she owned. ''This is all I have.''

''I'll loan you something.'' He swept past her and into the laundry room, returning with a gray T-shirt and shorts like the ones he wore.

Lynn jogged upstairs, changed and returned.

Sawyer's gaze scanned over her from top to toes. His jaw tightened and his nostrils flared. He jerked a nod. ''Put on the gloves.''

Ten minutes later she admitted that borrowing Sawyer's clothing was a mistake, especially on the heels of this morning in the kitchen when his every glance had been as hot as the glide of his hand over her skin.

Her body flickered to life, magnifying the slide of loose cotton against her breasts and the sweep of the oversize drawstring shorts around her thighs until she wanted to moan. Her reaction was ridiculous. Okay, so she was as sexually attracted to Sawyer as she had been years ago, but nothing had come of it then and nothing would now. This relationship was temporary, and she wanted to keep it that way. No more broken hearts for her.

From her kneeling position on the floor, she took out her frustrations on the rag in her hands, scrubbing away the stain Sawyer had applied to the waist-high wainscoting with his brush.

''Hey, easy there. Leave a little behind.'' Sawyer set

down his brush, knelt behind her and braced his left hand on her shoulder. He reached around her and covered her right hand with his, his thighs bracketing hers. If she leaned back even a smidgen his groin would cradle her buttocks. She felt surrounded, warm and very aware of herself as a woman.

"Like this. Just wipe off the excess. Applying a hand-rubbed finish takes a little practice, but you'll get the hang of it." He patiently demonstrated removing the excess stain with softer strokes along the wood grain.

The friction of his firm pectorals sliding against her shoulder blades made it difficult for Lynn to concentrate on technique. Her pulse drummed in her ears and her breath lodged in her chest. When she finally filled her lungs, it wasn't the wood stain she smelled. The scent of Sawyer's minty breath combined with his spicy cologne overwhelmed her senses and made her dizzy.

She couldn't blame the airlessness of the room on poor ventilation. Sawyer had positioned one fan in the open window to suck the stain fumes out and another at the entrance to force fresh air into the room. The breeze did nothing to cool her overheated skin.

"I'm sorry. I messed up," she wheezed, hoping he'd retreat to his end of the room.

He shrugged. She didn't see it; she *felt* it—the slide of his chest against her back. "Not a problem. I'll slap on more stain and nobody will ever know the difference."

He picked up his brush and applied more stain and moved back to the next section a short yard away. Her clenched muscles relaxed. Again he'd surprised her. Brett would have lectured her about how long it would take him to fix her mistake—not that he would ever have been caught doing manual labor in the first place. He paid others to do his dirty work.

Sawyer, she was beginning to discover, didn't have as much in common with his younger brother as she'd thought. He didn't belittle, and his generosity apparently didn't come with expectations of repayment. He took in stray, pregnant dogs…and stray, pregnant women. Sawyer Riggan was a genuine nice guy.

She touched her wrist to the ring hanging between her breasts. Don't get attached. Your judgment is faulty. Look how wrong you were last time. Shaking off the negative thoughts, she asked, "Why restore an old house when buying a new one would be so much easier?"

"We lost our house after Mom and Dad died and had to move into a cramped apartment. This neighborhood reminds me of the one Brett and I grew up in. There's nothing wrong with newer homes, but the old ones have a history and…" He shrugged.

"Character," she finished for him.

Their eyes met. "Exactly."

Lynn nodded. "I know what you mean. I love older homes, the mature gardens, the tall trees and the big yards."

"You are a plant lover, aren't you?" he asked with a crooked smile.

"I'm sorry. I can get rid of the house plants, if you like."

"Lynn, I like having green stuff in every room. It makes the house feel…like a home. Lived in. Cared for. Since you're such a green thumb, feel free to knock around outside in the garden."

"Don't you have a landscaping service?"

"Heck, no. What's the point of having a yard if you don't get out in it?"

Brett had hired a landscaping service and ordered her not to tamper with the expensive foliage he'd had installed. She hadn't been allowed to cut roses from her own yard. Luckily, she'd made friends with Lily the landscaper, and Lily had not only brought her blossoms each time she'd tended the yard, she'd taught Lynn tricks to keep her houseplants healthy. "But those beautiful flowers—"

"Came with the house. So did the blueberry bushes along the back edge of the property. We'll have a good crop come July. So why did you and Brett buy a new home?"

"He liked new things."

His brows dipped. "What about what you liked?"

"He was paying for the house, so he got to choose."

Sawyer set aside his brush. "I don't work that way. If you live here—even temporarily—then you have an interest in the decisions we make."

"You sound like you mean that." But talk, she'd learned the hard way, was cheap, and traps were subtly set.

"Lynn, I say what I mean, and I mean what I say. I expect people to show me the same courtesy."

She pushed a stray hair off her face with her knuckle. "I'll keep that in mind, but since I won't be here long, I don't want to sway your plans."

"Even after you leave, your child will be visiting." His gaze sharpened. "You smeared stain on your nose."

Grimacing, she looked at her hands encased in the plastic gloves. Messy. She dropped the dirty rag and searched for a cleaner one with no luck.

''Here, let me get it.'' On his knees, he edged closer, lifting the hem of his T-shirt as he approached. She caught a quick glimpse of the ridged muscles of his abdomen seconds before his belly brushed hers. Her breath hitched. One of his hands—decidedly cleaner than hers—settled on her nape, holding her stationary, while he used the other to blot the stain from her skin with his shirttail.

The heat of his stomach against hers caused a riotous response. She closed her eyes for fear he'd see her melting inside. When he stopped scrubbing but didn't release her, she slowly lifted her lids. His cobalt-blue gaze lasered in on hers, heated and then dropped to her mouth. Paralyzed by the sudden overwhelming need inside her, need which she saw reflected in Sawyer's eyes, she inhaled shakily and dampened her dry lips.

She wanted him to kiss her, to sweep her into that mind-numbing swirl of sensation where her worries vanished and she felt womanly and desirable. Only Sawyer could do that.

His fingers tightened in her hair, and his breath brushed her skin. She shivered and closed her eyes, and his mouth covered hers. His arm banded around her waist, pressing her hard against the hot length of him, and his tongue sliced through her lips to tangle with hers. He gently tugged on her ponytail, angling her head for a deeper penetration, and then he devoured her.

Her hands grew damp in the sticky plastic gloves. She wanted to peel them off and curl her fingers into Sawyer's supple flesh, but she kept her fists balled by her sides. Her skin tingled, and desire coiled in her belly. She ached for him to lay her down on the floor and make love to her right here on the rough, canvas drop cloth he'd spread across the hardwood floor. The knowledge shocked her. She couldn't afford to lose control. Panic stiffened her muscles and squeezed the air from her lungs. She shoved against his chest.

So much for platonic roommates.

Sawyer immediately released her. A muscle knotted in his jaw. He jerked his gaze back to the stain dripping down the wall. Tension radiated from every taut line of his body, and his breath rasped as harshly as her own.

Snatching up his paint brush, he put several yards between them. "If we want to finish in time for a swim before lunch we need to get back to work."

His rough baritone sent a flurry of goose bumps over her skin. Her heart pounded, but she nearly laughed out loud at the irony. He'd kissed her into a tailspin, then returned to work as usual. She swallowed hard and picked up the rag. Her hands trembled.

Sawyer wanted her, but he wasn't happy about it. Heaven help her, she wanted him, too, and the knowledge appalled her. She'd never been the kind of woman who gave her body lightly…except for that one time in the foyer. Until Sawyer, Brett had been her only lover, and what a nightmare that had been. Besides, if she made love with Sawyer again, she'd probably freeze up the way she always had before, and the experience would disappoint them both. If she doubted that, then all she had to do was read more of Brett's journal to find out what an abysmal example of womanhood she was.

She'd been young and stupid when she'd married Brett, but she was older and wiser now. She would keep her body and her heart to herself.

* * *

Living with Lynn was going to short-circuit his hard drive.

Sawyer laid the paint brush on the porch railing to dry in the sun. He reeked of stain and turpentine, and he couldn't wait to jump in the pool and rinse the odors from his skin. The cool water wouldn't hurt his libido, either. *That kiss.* Hell. Desire had tackled him like an NFL linebacker and ground him to a brainless pulp. Would he ever get enough of the taste of her?

She was off-limits to him, so why did his mind plague him with memories of the sweetness of her mouth and the softness of her bottom against his palms? Since he'd crossed the line, he couldn't seem to keep his mind on his side of the fence.

The back door opened, and Lynn, swaddled in an oversize towel, walked out, crossed the patio and dropped her towel on the concrete apron flanking the pool. He swallowed a groan. Trading in her flirty wardrobe for less-revealing clothing obviously hadn't included swapping her swimsuit. Sweat erupted on his skin, but the moisture had nothing to do with the summer heat and humidity and everything to do with the woman in front of him.

Lynn's lemon-yellow bikini top lifted and cupped her breasts the way his hands itched to do, and the high cut-bottom molded her tight butt like a spooning lover. Her muscles were slight, but firm and well formed. He traced the length of her endless legs with his gaze and then backtracked to her smooth belly. The hunger to have *his* child growing there surprised him, but he'd do right by the baby whether it proved to be his or his brother's.

The knot in his chest rivaled the tension in his groin.

He couldn't pry his eyes away as she arced into the pool and punctured the surface with almost no splash. She sliced through the water, quickly covering two laps. Maggie parked herself by Lynn's towel, apparently as fascinated by her new mistress as he.

Would Lynn like being pregnant? The wives of two of his team members had relished every aspect of pregnancies, and they'd shared more details than he'd wanted at the time. Swollen ankles. Shrinking bladders. Increased sex drive. *Like he needed to think about that right now.* The women had grabbed his hand and pressed it to their bellies, eager to share the power of their "little kickers."

Would Lynn let him feel her baby's movements? Since there was a chance the baby might be his, didn't that give him the right? He wanted to be a part of the pregnancy, the delivery and everything that came afterward. Would Lynn try to push him away?

Emptiness opened up inside him. His child wouldn't have the kind of family he'd had growing up. The love, the teasing, the sibling rivalry. As devastating as it had been to lose his parents and his baby brother, he couldn't regret the time they'd shared or the memories they'd made. Unless he and Lynn changed their agreement, then siblings were out of the question.

The desire to make love with Lynn butted against the hands-off sign that should be hanging around her neck. He'd wanted her from the day he'd met her, but getting his company off the ground had required days, sometimes weeks on the road. Before he'd left for California to clinch the contract guaranteed to keep his company afloat for years to come, he'd written a letter to Lynn explaining that once he landed the account, he hoped to see more of her. He'd given the letter to Brett to deliver, along with an apology for having to cancel at the last minute, but Lynn obviously hadn't been interested in waiting for him. He'd returned home two months later to find her married to his brother.

He still remembered the rock in his gut when Brett had grabbed her hand and waved her wedding band in his face. His plans for the future had crashed and burned at his brother's feet. He'd done his best to hide the fact that he lusted after his brother's wife. He'd dated so damned many women in the past four years that he couldn't even remember their names. Controlling his lust for Lynn had become easier when she'd turned into the kind of high-maintenance female he usually avoided, but now, with the old Lynn making a comeback, he was in serious trouble. Fresh-faced women with contagious grins and mile-long legs were his weakness.

He turned the water hose toward his face, drenching himself in frigid well water. After shutting off the spigot, he dried his face with his discarded T-shirt and then headed for the back door.

"Aren't you coming in?" Lynn called from the pool. She'd propped her arms on the edge of the pool. Her voice sounded breathless, no doubt winded from the half-dozen laps she'd swum.

"I'm going to check in with the office, and then I'll get a head start on clearing the garage."

She vaulted out of the water, startling Maggie back under the wrought-iron table. "I…I haven't decided where to put everything yet."

Snatching up her towel, she wound it around her lithe body, but not before the sight of her tight, pebbled nipples hit him like a punch in the gut. Her hair dripped in tangled strands over her shoulders, and she wore no makeup. He couldn't remember the last time he'd seen her unprimped before today. Had she ever looked better than she did now with her honey-colored skin damp, bare and glistening and with water droplets sparkling on her gold-tipped lashes? He didn't think so.

She looked young and innocent, too much—for his own his own piece of mind—like the girl he'd once hoped to claim for his own. "Finish your laps. I'll tackle the boxes while you're out this afternoon."

She hurried across the patio and stepped between him and the door. "Sawyer, I have personal stuff packed in them. I'd really rather deal with all of it myself."

She focused on a spot over his left shoulder rather than meet his gaze, leaving him to wonder if the kiss had made her uncomfortable, or if there was something more.

Rivulets of water snaked from her hair over her shoulders and breast bone to disappear into the shadowy space between her breasts. His pulse accelerated. He swiped a hand over his chin. "You shouldn't lift anything heavy. Tell me where you want the boxes, and I'll move them for you while you're gone."

"I'm pregnant, not injured."

"Until you see a doctor and find out exactly what your limitations are, I'd rather play it safe."

"Sawyer—"

"This one's nonnegotiable, Lynn."

She looked ready to argue and then sighed. "Just put everything in the nursery. I'll dry off and make lunch."

He reached for the doorknob, but her touch on his arm stopped him. "Sawyer, just so you know, I would never consciously do anything to hurt this baby. Things may not have turned out exactly how I planned, but I'm looking forward to having someone to love."

Her gentle smile and the protective hand she placed on her tummy parked a lump the size of his SUV in his throat.

She wasn't talking about loving him.

Seven

It seemed eerily appropriate to hide her darkest secrets at the witching hour of midnight. Rising from her perch on one of the boxes Sawyer had stacked in the nursery, Lynn clutched Brett's journal to her chest, slinked back into her bedroom and quietly closed the door.

The journal made her feel exposed and unwanted, but until she could unravel Brett's weird notes she couldn't throw it away. If he had money stashed somewhere, then she needed to find it to cover his debts. It was frustrating because it was almost as if he'd written in some kind of code that only he could understand. She wished she could ask for Sawyer's help in deciphering the puzzling remarks, but doing so would reveal all of her faults. The old brass bed creaked when she pushed the book all the way to the sagging spot between her mattress and box spring.

The hour she'd spent with the journal had rattled her

nerves and made her stomach churn. She'd never get to sleep in this state. A glass of milk might help. Opening the door to the hall as quietly as possible, she winced at the hinges' squeak and then tiptoed down the stairs and into the kitchen. While her milk heated she checked on Maggie. The dog, curled on a pile of blankets in the laundry room, looked as restless as Lynn felt. After filling her mug, Lynn leaned against the counter, sipped and grimaced. Nasty stuff but supposedly good for insomnia and the little one she carried.

A shaft of light shone through the partially open door of Sawyer's study, drawing her like a moth to a flame. Sawyer, wearing the khaki shorts and polo shirt he'd put on before dinner, sat on the leather sofa with a large open book propped on his knees. A half tumbler of dark liquid sat on the coffee table beside a stack of more large books. Photo albums? He lifted his head and stilled before she could make herself scarce. His gaze raked from her face to her toes before slowly tracking back up to her eyes. Her body stirred.

A lock of dark hair had tumbled over his forehead, and beard stubble covered his jaw. "Trouble sleeping?"

The gravelly edge to his voice gave her goose bumps. She crossed her arms over her chest to hide her tightened nipples. Why hadn't she worn her robe? Her silky, short, slip gown revealed too much. A wise woman would retreat to her room. "I came to get a glass of milk to help me sleep. That nap this afternoon confused my body clock."

That was only part of the story. Watching the estate salesman cart off her belongings that afternoon had been difficult, like hammering the final nail in the coffin of her dreams. Four years wasted. The contents of those two rooms upstairs represented her entire life and all her worldly possessions. Not much to show for twenty-three years.

Leave Sawyer alone with his memories. Go back to bed.

Sawyer lifted the tumbler, drained it and looked down at the album in his lap. "He's been gone a month."

His pain-laced voice halted her retreat. "I know."

"This is his kindergarten graduation." He gestured to the picture in front of him.

Lynn wanted to escape, but Sawyer was hurting. He wanted to remember Brett as much as she wanted to forget his brother and the hard lessons he'd taught her. Talking about Brett was a natural part of the grieving process, and maybe by letting Sawyer talk she could understand why she'd fallen for Brett, how she'd been fooled by him. The knowledge could keep her from repeating her mistakes.

Edging closer, she stood by his side and looked over his shoulder at the grinning picture of Brett. Even then his eyes had danced with devilry, with promises of fun and laughter—promises he hadn't kept after the wedding. She sank down on the sofa beside Sawyer, keeping several inches between them, but his scent, mingled with the tang of bourbon and the warmth of his body reached out to her. She gulped her milk, hoping to settle her agitated stomach.

Sawyer turned the page. "This is the day he started first grade."

Brett looked so zestful and carefree with his white-blond hair. Beside him, Sawyer looked every inch the protective older brother with his serious expression and neatly combed dark hair. Would her child resemble one of them? The shame of not knowing which man had fathered her baby heated her cheeks. She wasn't promiscuous, but not being able to name the father of her child made her feel that way.

She tamped down the unpleasant feeling. ''How old were you?''

''Twelve. There are—there *were* six years between us.'' Sawyer turned the pages, adding a line of explanation here and short story there. They finished one photo album and moved to another as the hour passed. Sawyer's love for his brother was evident on every page and in the tales he told, but the man he described wasn't the one she'd woken up to after her marriage.

Brett had possessed a darker side that he'd hidden from his brother, and she wouldn't tell Sawyer because she didn't want his memories of his brother to be tainted. Family was the most important thing in the world, and she'd learned the hard way that when memories of loved ones are all you have left, those memories need to be the type to keep you warm at night instead of the kind that haunted your dreams.

The Brett Sawyer described was the one Lynn had fallen in love with, and she felt a little less stupid knowing she wasn't the only one Brett had fooled. When he'd been sweeping her off her feet, Brett had shown her nothing but his charming side. She'd fallen in love with the idea of love and with a man who'd promised to make her dreams of home, hearth and family come true. But it had all been sheer fantasy. After the wedding he'd changed. She'd excused his neglect first by blaming it on the pressure of final exams and his upcoming graduation, then on his new job. And then she'd realized that the problem was her. She'd disappointed him in some way.

The photo albums revealed an ideal family, one that traveled and played together. The Riggans' obvious solidarity made her heart ache for those kinds of bonds—the involved parents, the dedicated sibling—for her child, but she'd never have them if she and Sawyer stuck with their marriage-of-convenience agreement. Her child would be a lonely, only child like her. Could she and Sawyer remain friends for their child's sake after they divorced? Could they have a family without love to complicate things?

"I envy you," she confessed.

He jerked his gaze to hers in surprise. "Why?"

"Because you have these." She touched an album. "After my mother died, my father was so hurt and angry he burned our pictures. I only had Mom for eleven years, and so many of my memories have faded. You had twenty-two years with your parents, and when you lost them, you had these and your brother to help you get through your grief."

"You told me your memories were here." He brushed her temple with a featherlight touch, and her skin prickled. "What do you remember most?"

"When I close my eyes, I can still see her smile. My mother was always happy and usually singing. My father would come home from work tired and beaten down, but my mom always put a smile on his face. After she died, I tried to do the same, but I couldn't." She'd never admitted her failure before and didn't know why she did now. Maybe it was the lateness of the hour or Sawyer's willingness to share his own memories.

He covered the hand she had fisted on her knee, silently offering support. Her throat tightened. "What do you remember most about your mom?"

A sad smile curved his lips. "Questions. She always asked questions. Maybe it was the university professor in her, but she made you look beyond the surface. We were never allowed to accept anything at face value. We had to know *why* it was that way.''

''Which explains how you became a computer expert.''

''Wanting to know how things work was only part of it. The rest was a career decision. You already know Carter and I roomed together during college. What you don't know is that he's like another brother to me. We were both computer geeks. We'd planned to get our degrees and join the U.S. Marines together and let the government turn us into computer experts. We pictured ourselves as computer-age secret agents.''

Another facet she hadn't known about the man she'd married. ''I didn't know you'd been in the military.''

''I never made it. My parents died on the way home from my graduation dinner. Carter and I were supposed to enlist the following week, but I backed out. I needed to take care of Brett.'' The clipped delivery of the words hinted at emotions he wasn't sharing.

''I doubt Carter faults you for that.''

His jaw set. ''I'd promised to stand beside Carter, and I don't believe in breaking promises. The company he operates now was supposed to be our company. We both followed our dreams, but separately instead of as a team.''

''You could hardly go off to fight in who-knows-where and have Brett lose you, too, Sawyer. You were all he had left.''

''My fiancée didn't agree. She took off when I refused to make him a ward of the court.''

Lynn turned her hand over and laced her fingers through his. ''I'm sorry.''

He shrugged. ''If she'd loved me enough, she would

have stayed. Love doesn't quit when the going gets tough."

Sawyer closed the album and returned it to the stack on the coffee table. "Our child will have two parents who love him, and we'll make memories that count."

"I know, but it won't be the same when we're dividing holidays and shuffling *her* back and forth between us."

His eyes twinkled and her insides warmed. "You know something I don't know?"

"No, but I don't know anything about raising boys, so I'm hoping for a girl."

"And I don't know anything about raising girls. I guess we'll have to learn together." The tenderness of his gaze hypnotized her and made her wish for what would never be.

A mournful howl raised the hair on the back of Lynn's neck. She sprang to her feet. "It's Maggie. She sounds like she's in pain."

She raced to the laundry room, and Sawyer, hot on her heels, bumped into her when she jerked to a halt on the threshold. He grasped her waist to steady them both.

Lynn's breath caught at the warmth of his touch through her thin gown and at the wonder unfolding in front of her. "She's having her puppies."

The first puppy slipped free. Maggie licked and cleaned it. Sawyer made a choking sound behind her. Lynn looked over her shoulder. He looked nauseated. "Are you okay?"

He grimaced and swallowed hard. "Yeah. I don't know anything about dogs in labor. Do you?"

"No. Do you think we're supposed to help her?"

In other circumstances she would have laughed at his

horrified expression. "I have no idea. I'll call Rick's vet."

"It's one in the morning. The vet's office is closed."

"I'll leave a message with his answering service, but there's no telling how long it will take for the vet to call back. Boot up my computer. We'll do a Web search for instructions on delivering puppies."

"Shouldn't I stay with Maggie?"

"I think we should know what we're doing before we interfere. Give me two minutes to make the call, and then I'll help you search."

Lynn raced back to Sawyer's study and turned on the computer. She pulled up an article and hit the print button.

Sawyer returned. "I left a message. The operator didn't think birth was an emergency since Maggie's not a pedigreed pooch."

"I found instructions." She nodded to the pages spewing out of the printer. Another howl from Maggie made them both jump.

Sawyer rubbed the back of his neck and paced as he read the article. His gaze met hers. "We can do this."

"I'm glad to hear it."

Two hours later Sawyer stood beside Lynn in the laundry room watching the fifth slimy little puppy come into the world. Unlike the last four, Maggie didn't immediately wash this one. After one sniff, she ignored it.

"Come on, Maggie," Lynn urged. Her grip on Sawyer's hand tightened. He didn't remember when she'd taken his hand, just that it seemed right to be holding hers while they watched the birth. "What are we going to do? Do you think it's alive?"

They'd read online about stillbirths, and he'd been prepared…or so he thought. He willed the tiny creature to wiggle and then it did. Ignoring his protesting stomach, he moved forward, picked up the slippery pup, and laid it at Maggie's paws. Maggie nosed it away. His gut clenched, and he looked over his shoulder. Lynn's eyes silently beseeched him to fix this, and his gut knotted.

"Go back to that Web site and find out what to do with an abandoned puppy."

Worry clouded her eyes. "You think she's rejecting it?"

He offered the fragile baby to Maggie again, and again she pushed it away. "Yes."

He broke the sac enclosing the pup and used the edge of the blanket to wipe him clean. The pup made tiny, helpless noises and Sawyer's heart clenched. It was just a dog, damn it. Why was he choking up?

The phone rang and Lynn answered it. "It's the vet."

"About time. Tell him what's going on. Ask him to walk me through whatever I have to do."

Lynn relayed the information, leading him through cleaning and warming the pup. Her expression made him feel as if he were accomplishing a most heroic feat. He didn't want to let her down or remind her that the odds were against them. He wanted to save the puppy for her.

When she finished the call, Sawyer rose, placed the tiny critter in her palms and then cradled her hands in his. Tears welled up in her eyes, and a lump formed in his throat.

He stroked the pup's stubby little nose and ran his finger over his wet rust-colored fur. "The Supercenter is open all night. I'll take the list the doc gave us and go buy supplies."

She chewed her bottom lip and looked at him. Concern darkened her eyes and furrowed her forehead. "I'll keep an eye on this little fella and Maggie, too. I can't believe she didn't want her baby."

He shrugged off the residual bitterness. His gaze dropped to Lynn's belly. He couldn't imagine giving up his child. "It happens all the time. Puppies, people. Brett was adopted. His mother decided she couldn't handle him. She dumped him in a church when he was two."

She gasped. "I didn't know. He never said anything."

"I hope he didn't remember being unwanted. He was almost three when he came to live with us. We were damned glad to have him, and we tried to make it up to him."

"But you two were so close. I never would have guessed…"

"There's nothing I wouldn't have done for Brett. Adopting him made my mother happy. She'd been pretty torn up by several miscarriages and she wasn't able to have more kids." He washed his hands and snatched up the shopping list. "Keep him warm. I'll be as quick as I can."

Sawyer grabbed his keys and disappeared. Lynn sat in the darkness cradling the puppy. Brett had been abandoned. Was that why he never cuddled her, never touched her and never loved her?

A steady thump woke Lynn. She snuggled into her pillow and tried to ignore the sound, but her pillow wasn't soft. Neither was her bed. Her legs were cramped and bent and… She opened her gritty eyes and blinked. She wasn't in her creaky brass bed.

"Ready to go upstairs?" Sawyer's quiet baritone banished the remnants of grogginess from her brain. She jerked upright on the sofa. She'd been asleep, curled against Sawyer's chest with his arm draping her shoulders and the puppy in her lap. Only the dim light from the front hall penetrated the darkness. Her heart raced and her skin flushed.

"I'm sorry. I didn't mean to mash you." She hid her embarrassment by checking the pup's tiny warm body and repositioning the towel and hot water bottle. The last thing she remembered was Sawyer passing her the puppy after he'd fed and massaged it with such gentleness that her heart had melted.

"You didn't mash me. Are you ready to go to bed?" His husky voice made her wonder if he'd also been asleep.

She licked her dry lips. "No. I'd like to stay with the puppy. The vet said the first twenty-four hours are critical. What time is it?"

"Almost six." He tucked a lock of hair behind her ear. The gentle touch of his fingertip made her shiver. "Lynn, you're dead on your feet. Go to bed. I'll keep an eye on the pup."

Sawyer had stepped in and taken control tonight. He'd clearly been a little nauseated by the entire birth process, but he hadn't hesitated when the pup needed help. Would he be as bold and fearless with their child?

Their child. Her heart skipped a beat. Until tonight she'd considered the baby she carried to be hers and hers alone. Sure, she'd thought about having Sawyer around as a father figure in a vague sort of way, but she hadn't allowed herself to visualize him parenting her child. He'd be so gentle, so loving. Was she wrong in refusing to try to form a real family with him? Could she and Sawyer replicate the live-together, love-together family Sawyer had grown up in, and if so, could she keep her heart intact?

He took the sleeping puppy from her and set it in a towel-lined box on the hearth. Her heart softened at the careful way he handled the fragile puppy. "He's adorable."

"Yeah and he's a fighter—a real trooper." The pride in his voice made her smile.

"Trooper. That's what we should name him." Lynn touched his arm. "He would have died if not for you."

He shrugged and she laughed. "You don't want to be a hero? Well, too bad. You are." She closed the distance between them and kissed his cheek. Her breast brushed his biceps. She felt the contact deep in her womb.

He sucked in a sharp breath. His arm banded around her shoulders holding her when she would have pulled away. Their gazes locked, and awareness arched between them. Her skin prickled from head to toe. The banked fire in his eyes made her pulse pound and the tender place between her thighs tingle. She wanted him to kiss her, wanted him to make her feel the way that only he could make her feel. Desirable. Wanted. She dampened her lips and swallowed to ease the dryness in her mouth.

He cupped her jaw in one large, warm hand and leaned forward until only an inch separated their mouths. "Lynn, tell me you want this," he whispered roughly.

She couldn't speak, so she touched her lips to his. Her lids fluttered closed.

He groaned and slid his fingers into her hair, curling and flexing them at her nape. A shiver skipped down her spine and goose bumps swept over her flesh. His mouth pressed down on hers, and the slick heat of his tongue parted her lips, making her dizzy with desire. He sampled her mouth, teasing her, tempting her to reciprocate, and then he suckled her tongue when she dared to kiss him back. She clutched his shoulders for support, stroking and kneading his taut muscles.

His free hand settled at her waist, scorching through her thin gown as he stroked her hip, her thigh. Easing her backward on the sofa, he stretched out beside her, aligning her body with his. Their bare legs tangled, and his thigh slid between her knees. His wiry leg hairs teased her skin, and his arousal, thick, hard and hot, branded her hipbone with scalding insistence. The tension in her lower belly increased. She twined her arms behind his neck and bowed her back, pressing against him in an attempt to ease the excruciating emptiness yawning inside her. His hungry kiss intensified until she could barely breathe.

He tunneled a hand beneath the hem of her gown, tracing an agonizingly slow upward path with his fingers. Cupping her breast, he scraped his thumbnail over the sensitive tip, and she thought she'd go up in flames. She yanked her mouth free to gasp for air. Sawyer's touch was gentle—so gentle it made her hungry and impatient for more. She pushed herself greedily into his palm and touched her lips to his throat, licking him and savoring the saltiness of his skin on her tongue and letting the scent of him fill her senses.

With a groan, he eased his hand beneath her panties and found her wet center. The pleasure was extreme, unbearably so. She bit her lip, trying to hold back the moans multiplying in her chest, and then he plunged his fingers deep inside her, and she couldn't keep silent. His slick fingers circled on the tender seat of her passion, and she bucked involuntarily against his tormenting touch. With skillful strokes he wound her tighter and tighter until she snapped, crying out as ecstasy rippled through her. She'd feared her passionate response the first time had been a fluke somehow connected to her unstable emotional state, but that wasn't the case tonight.

Sawyer soothed and petted her, sipping from her lips and kissing her brow, and then he eased his hands from her body and clutched the hem of her gown in his fists. He tugged the fabric over her head and sat back to study what he'd uncovered. Even in the dimly lit room she felt self-conscious and lifted her hands to cover herself.

"You're beautiful." His hoarse words stopped her.

She almost believed him. *Almost.* But she'd had years of Brett telling her that her breasts weren't large enough to turn on a real man. Desire ebbed. She turned her head and the chill of the night air crept over her.

"Lynn, look at me." His command made the fine hairs on her body stand at attention. Afraid she might see disappointment in his eyes, she hesitated before lifting her gaze to his. He looked as if he could eat her up bite by tantalizing bite. "No regrets this time."

Surprised, she blinked at him. Did that mean he still wanted her? *Her* with the barely B-cup breasts and less-than-plump lips? The desire dilating his pupils, flaring his nostrils and making his chest rise and fall like a bellows said he did. A dark flush swept his cheekbones, and a nerve twitched in his jaw. He looked like a man teetering on the edge of control, trembling with the force of holding back. *For her.*

A spark of womanly confidence reignited the embers within her. She lifted her hand and stroked her fingertips over the dark stubble bristling his jaw. "No regrets."

Blood pooled in Sawyer's groin, and his chest tightened to the point where he could barely breathe. Slow down. Take it easy. Don't rush her this time.

Easier said than done. His heart hammered against his rib cage, and a ravenous hunger urged him to feast. Now.

He stood, hauling his shirt over his head, but he couldn't tear his gaze from Lynn. Her lips were damp and swollen, and hunger burned in her blue eyes. Her breasts were firm and round with tightly puckered rosy tips, the perfect size to fill his hands and leave no waste. Shadowy blue veins showed through her milky skin, and he couldn't wait to trace each one with his tongue. His fingers flexed in anticipation and his mouth watered.

He dropped back down on the sofa beside her and fought the demons inside that urged him to drive them both insane as quickly as possible. He could always take it slowly *next time.*

Beneath the glide of his fingertip, her bottom lip was as soft as silk and damp from his kisses. His hand trembled when he stroked down the cord of her neck, bumping over the fine gold chain she wore on his way to the pulse fluttering wildly at the base of her throat. The chain had fallen behind her, becoming trapped between her body and the arm of the sofa. The gold links cut into her delicate skin. He dragged his finger back up, hooked it beneath the necklace and tugged.

The dismay in her eyes registered a split second before the liberated charm hanging from the necklace dropped between her breasts.

A wedding band. Brett's wedding band.

A chill washed over him, immediately extinguishing the raging fire in his blood. There were areas where a man didn't want to play second string to his brother.

Bed topped the list. He clenched his fists and sucked in a sobering breath to stave off the monster of jealousy.

Sharing the pup's birth tonight, having Lynn curl up and sleep in his arms had made him want what he couldn't have. Lynn was grieving and on the rebound. The ring said it all. Her heart still belonged to Brett.

She clutched her gown to her chest. ''Sawyer, I'm sorry.''

Sorry for what? Pretending he was his brother?

The regret in her eyes opened the acid floodgates in his stomach. Anger and hurt raged inside him. How stupid was he to fall for Lynn a second time? And just like before, Brett got the girl.

He shoved himself to his feet. ''I'm not into threesomes. Don't come to me again until Brett's not the one you see when you close your eyes.''

Eight

The puppy was missing. Instantly awake, Lynn sprang up in the bed, shoved the hair out of her eyes and turned on the bedside lamp. It wasn't her imagination or a trick of her tired eyes. Trooper's box wasn't beside her bed.

Sawyer must have taken him, but she hadn't heard him come into her room. Had he stood beside her bed and watched her sleep? Goose bumps rose on her skin. She shoved back the covers, raced through her morning rituals and yanked on red shorts and a matching top. She ran down the stairs, checked on Maggie and her pups and then stopped by the patio doors. Through the glass she saw a lone swimmer slicing through the pool with swift, efficient strokes. The puppy lay curled in his box on top of the wrought-iron patio table. Her worry drained and she gave a relieved sigh. She'd been afraid something had happened to the pup. He wasn't beyond the danger zone yet.

Lynn poured herself a glass of juice and went outside. She sank into a chair beside Trooper, sipped her juice and watched Sawyer swim. Her stomach tightened. If they were going to have an honest relationship, then she had to explain about the ring. It wasn't fair to let Sawyer believe she'd found him deficient in any way. She knew from personal experience how debilitating that emotion could be.

After another fifteen minutes, Sawyer heaved himself from the pool. Water cascaded over his wide shoulders, his deep chest and his muscular abdomen, molding his brief black trunks to the contours of his masculinity before sluicing down his legs.

Lynn's breath caught and her pulse raced. Her mouth dried and her breasts tingled. How could merely looking at this man make her feel feminine and fluttery? And why had her body chosen to awaken so easily for Sawyer when during her first marriage she would have given anything for even a fraction of this arousal? The more she'd worried about her lack of response to Brett the more tense she'd become.

Sawyer stalked toward her, stopping a short yard away. "Did you get enough rest?"

"Yes. I'm sorry I slept so late."

He reached for his towel. His gaze traced her face, making her wish she'd taken the time to do more than slash on lipstick and comb her hair. "We were up most of the night with the furball. You needed to catch up."

She tried not to stare as he dragged the fabric over his skin, but the bunching and flexing of his muscles fascinated her. The dark hair on his chest sprang into tight curls as it dried.

She wrapped her fingers around the edge of her seat and cleared her throat. "Sawyer, about last night—"

His face closed up.

''I need to explain.'' She took a bracing breath. ''I wasn't thinking about Brett when you kissed me.''

His lips flattened to a thin line. He leaned his hip against the table and folded his arms over his chest, but despite his casual pose, every tense muscle in his body belied his attempt to appear calm. A nerve jerked in his freshly shaven jaw, and he stared so intently that she could see the lighter shards in the cobalt blue of his eyes.

She smoothed a hand over her hair and took a shaky breath. ''I wear… I *wore* the necklace for only one reason—to remind me that this is a marriage of convenience. Neither of us went into it expecting hearts and flowers, but I…''

She'd faced rejection so many times in her life she feared this confession would lead to another one. First her father, so blinded by pain, had shut down his emotions and sealed himself off from her after her mother's death, and then her high school friends had turned on her when the scandal about her father had broken. Next Sawyer had tired of her, and then Brett had decided she wasn't worth the effort. She felt exposed, but she had to make Sawyer understand.

''But you…?'' he prompted.

''I like you, Sawyer. I like your kindness, your friends and the fact that you painted my bedroom to match my grandmother's quilt. I think it's amazingly generous that you're willing to baby-sit for a friend's pregnant dog and to become a surrogate dad to an abandoned puppy. I love that you put your loyalty to your brother ahead of everything else. In fact, I like everything about you.''

Her heart raced and she thought she might hyperventilate. She braced herself for his reaction, but other than a slight narrowing of his eyes and flaring of his nostrils he didn't respond. She plowed on, but her throat closed up and she had trouble forcing out the words. "You need to know that I don't plan to fall in love again. *Ever.* I don't need another broken heart. I wore the ring to remind me that love is…complicated. But I wasn't pretending you were Brett. You're so—" superior to Brett in every way "—different from Brett."

She pressed her cold hands to her cheeks, exhaled and tried again. "I'm sorry. I'm rambling. What I'm trying to say is that I think we could have a good marriage based on mutual respect and friendship. I'd like to try to give this child the kind of upbringing you had."

Without breaking eye contact, he pushed off from the table and moved closer. Leaning forward, he braced himself on the arms of her chair. Her stomach dropped and her palms dampened.

His sharp gaze held her captive. "Would falling in love with your husband be such a bad thing?"

"Yes. Love ends." And it ends painfully with hard words that couldn't be taken back or forgotten.

His eyes softened. He knelt in front of her. "It doesn't have to, Lynn. My parents had twenty-five years of marriage and died loving each other."

He brushed the hair off her cheek with the back of his hand, tucked a strand behind her ear and curled his long fingers around her nape. His thumb settled over the pulse galloping at the base of her throat. "What do you say we keep the doors open and see where this year takes us?"

The heat in his eyes turned her muscles into liquid and robbed every speck of moisture from her mouth.

Goose bumps marched across her skin, and her nipples tightened painfully. She couldn't breathe and barely managed to nod in response to his question.

He rose, tugged her to her feet and slowly lowered his head until she could feel the warmth of his breath on her lips. He rested his forehead on hers and nuzzled her nose with his. Their mouths brushed, butterfly light, parted and touched again. And then he drew back until his cobalt gaze lasered into hers.

"I want to make love with you, Lynn, but only if you're certain you have no doubt who's sharing your bed."

Her heart thumped against her rib cage. She had doubts, but not the kind he meant. Her doubts were personal. What if she froze up, became dead from the neck down and disappointed them both? It hadn't happened last night or in the foyer, but those were two incidences versus four years of painful and humiliating misery.

She swallowed hard. Could they be lovers—not *in love,* but lovers? Yes, of course. Although she was only twenty-three, she was mature for her age. She could handle a purely physical relationship, and as long as she kept her heart tucked safely away then she wouldn't be hurt when it ended. "I could never confuse you with your brother."

She tipped her head back and parted her lips, but instead of the devouring, thought-blocking kiss she wanted—*needed*—he nestled his face in the side of her neck and inhaled deeply.

"You smell delicious...like honeysuckles and summertime." He opened his mouth over her pulse point, bathing her with his tongue.

"It's my—" her breath hitched and her stomach clenched when he nipped her "—shower gel."

"You use it all over?" he asked against her jawline. His chest brushed hers, teasing her sensitive breasts.

She couldn't stop trembling. "Yes."

A groan rumbled in his chest and then he captured her face with both hands and took her mouth with such scorching intensity that she felt woozy and weak-kneed. The persuasive pressure of his lips coaxed hers apart for the seductive invasion of his tongue. His hands swept down her spine to cup her buttocks and pull her flush against him. The hard evidence of his need pressed her belly, drawing her blood like a magnet draws iron filings. She shivered, slid her arms around his waist and curled and flexed her fingers into the muscles of his back like a cat being stroked. The dampness of his swim trunks saturated her shorts, but she didn't care. The kiss turned carnal, feverish.

Sawyer tugged her shirttail from her shorts and tunneled his hands beneath the fabric to encircle her waist. His fingers burned her skin from her spine to the bottom of her rib cage. He stroked upward, and the muscles of her midriff contracted involuntarily. With a flick of his fingers, the front closure of her bra snapped open and his hot palms cradled her. Breaking the kiss, she gasped.

Breath whistled between Sawyer's teeth. He snatched up the towel and wrapped it around his hips, but the thick material couldn't camouflage his condition. "Let's take this upstairs. I'll get the pup."

Uncertain and afraid that she might be making a huge mistake, she hesitated. Sawyer must have read her mind. Wedging the box beneath one arm, he caught her hand in his and led her up the stairs and into her room. He carefully set the puppy's box on the floor and faced her.

"Second thoughts?" His gaze held hers.

Making love with Sawyer could move her one step closer to having the family she'd always dreamed of. "No."

He stepped closer. His hips nudged hers, and then he brushed his lips across her brow, her temple. His hands skated from her waist to her stiff nipples, where he circled and teased until she whimpered. He peeled her shirt over her head, revealing her unclasped red bra, and groaned.

"Lynn, I don't want to rush you." His husky voice and searing eyes made her skin hot and tingly. Brett had never looked at her with such intense hunger, not even the first time.

"Rush me," she whispered. Please rush me. Don't give me time to think of the past or worry about the future. Don't give me time to wonder if I'm making another mistake.

And then contrarily, he did exactly the opposite. He eased her bra from her shoulders, inch by excruciating inch, and then stepped back, catching her hands in his and breathing heavily. He backed toward her bed, sat down and pulled her between his spread knees. His hands shook as he leisurely traced her areolas with blunt fingertips, and then he dipped his head and repeated the process with the scorching tip of his tongue.

She'd never experienced this deliberate, intense buildup of passion before, and it was driving her crazy. Shifting on her feet, she squeezed her thighs together, trying to ease the ache. She dug her nails into his shoulders, but he wouldn't be rushed. He feasted first on one breast and then the other, licking, nibbling and finally drawing her into his mouth. Her knees buckled. He caught her in his arms and kissed her deeply, hungrily.

The world tilted and spun. But the quilt against her back grounded her in reality as he laid her down on the bed. She and Sawyer were going to make love. Need twisted inside her, making her eager and impatient for the act in a way that she'd never been before. This wasn't duty, and it wasn't the desperate act of a woman on the verge of a nervous breakdown. This was elemental—man and woman and their driving hunger for each other.

It wasn't love. She wouldn't let it be.

He reached for the button on her shorts. Her skin jumped at the brush of his knuckles against her navel, and then the waistband gave way. The zipper quickly followed. He eased the fabric down her legs and over her ankles, leaving her red bikini panties behind. For several seconds he drank in the sight of her in the bright flaw-revealing sunlight bathing her bed.

She curled her fingers into her palms and fought the urge to cover herself, focusing instead on the hard ridge expanding behind his zipper. That telling sign, combined with the smoldering desire in his eyes told her Sawyer wasn't cataloging her faults.

He knelt on the mattress, bracing himself above her on straight arms. Slowly he lowered until his chest hair tantalized her breasts, her belly. She arched her back to intensify the contact. He captured her mouth. One mind-boggling kiss led to another and another. He abandoned her mouth to leave a trail of hot, openmouthed kisses from her neck to her collarbone and then her breasts. He sipped the crests, laved the undersides. Traveling lower with each sip and nip, he forged a path down her breastbone to her belly where he rimmed her navel with his tongue as he inched her panties down her legs.

After the wisp of fabric cleared her ankles, he cupped

her buttocks in his warm hands and descended farther still. Her muscles locked. She'd never experienced this part of lovemaking before, but then he gently parted her curls and found just the right spot to preempt her objections.

Lynn clenched her fists in the quilt, and when he focused on a particularly magical area, she dug her fingers into his hair, certain she couldn't withstand such extreme pleasure. Sawyer intensified his ministrations until her climax rocked her with such force that she called out his name and her body bowed off the bed.

He planted successive kisses on her tummy, her breasts, her lips, and then he stood, quickly stripping off his swim trunks to reveal the blatant thrust of his masculinity.

She had another moment of doubt. The man was perfect. Why settle for her? But she shoved the negative thought aside, sat up and reached for him. She curled her fingers around his thick, silky shaft and bent her head.

"Stop," he ground out, tangling his fingers in her hair and halting her one scant inch from her target.

She frowned up at him. His jaw muscles bunched, and the tendons of his neck strained as if he were in pain. "Don't you need me to...?"

His passion-clouded eyes locked with hers. "Baby, if I get any closer to your mouth it's going to be over. As it is, your breath on my skin is about to kill me."

His rough voice made her shiver, and surprise made her fingers go lax. "But—"

"Another time. Lie back and let me love you, Lynn."

She fought to catch her breath, eased back and extended her hand. He yanked the quilt from beneath her, pressed her back onto the cool sheets with a scorching kiss and then knelt between her thighs. Bracing himself on one arm, he leaned forward until his thick shaft probed her entrance, testing her dampness. He stroked her where their bodies would soon join, and her breath came in jerky gasps as tension built. Her lids fluttered closed.

"Don't."

She blinked at him in confusion.

"Don't close your eyes." He lowered his head and brushed his lips against hers. She'd never kissed with her eyes open, and it was a strangely intimate feeling as if he could see into her soul. The soft sweep of his lips over hers sent a tingle through her and weighted her lids. She fought to keep them open but lost the battle when his tongue traced the inside of her bottom lip. "Look at me and say my name."

Although her pulse pounded and her body craved his, her heart ached. How could he believe she'd be thinking of Brett when he was so much more? She curled her hands around his hips and urged him closer. "Sawyer, please. I need you."

He thrust deep and groaned, "Again."

Her memory of that night in the foyer hadn't done him justice. His thickness filled her more than she was accustomed to, but her body adjusted and welcomed his. Making love with her eyes open was a new experience, but Sawyer's eyes reflected the same passion and need that raged inside her, and it empowered her. He wanted *her,* needed *her.*

She chanted his name and lifted her hips, meeting him stroke for stroke. Tension coiled inside her, tightening until her muscles trembled under the strain. She dug her nails into his back and pulled him down, hungering for his mouth. The wiry curls on his chest teased her, incited her, and then she snapped, convulsing with wave after wave of pleasure. He swallowed her cries and pounded into her as his own release undulated through him.

He collapsed to his elbows. Their sweat-slicked chests and bellies rose and fell in unison as each panted for breath. Warm and sated, Lynn held him close, stroking the damp skin on his back and savoring the fact that she hadn't been cold or unresponsive. She felt whole—like a real woman.

He rolled sideways and reluctantly, she let him go, but instead of shutting her out and going straight to the shower as she expected, he pulled her into his arms, tucked her head beneath his chin and held her close. His fingertips skated down her spine with a touch so light that the fine hairs rose on her skin. The need she'd thought he'd satisfied rekindled.

With every touch and every scorching look, Sawyer made her feel sexy and desirable instead of inadequate. Hope filled her heart, and she was very afraid that she might be setting herself up for another heartbreak.

If he hadn't known better, Sawyer would have sworn Lynn lacked sexual experience. She wasn't a virgin by any means, but she'd seemed surprised by ninety percent of what they'd done in the past three hours.

He tucked his T-shirt into his jeans as questions rolled through his mind like a summer thunderstorm. It was obvious she knew how to give pleasure, but she'd seemed surprised to receive it. The thought took him in a direction he didn't want to go, making the muscles between his shoulder blades knot and raising questions for which he didn't want answers. He couldn't think about Lynn with Brett—not when his skin still smelled of her and not when he still battled the guilt over sharing the future his brother should have had with her. The water in the bathroom turned off and the shower door clicked open. He shoved the unpalatable feelings aside and leaned against the doorjamb to enjoy the view.

She hadn't spotted him yet. She stood in the glass shower cubicle surrounded by a cloud of steam. Her damp skin glistened in the sunlight filtering through the lace curtains. One slender arm reached for the towel hanging on the rack. She snagged the fabric and dragged it over her hair, her neck, her back. Her breasts jiggled with each move, quickening his pulse and heating his groin. Guilt kicked him in the teeth when he noticed the spots of beard burn scattered about her fair skin and the love bite on her neck.

She stepped out onto the bath mat and bent to dry her long legs. He groaned at the view of her sweetly rounded hips. Startled, she straightened abruptly and shielded herself from his hungry gaze with the towel. "Did you need something?"

"No, I'm just enjoying the view."

A blush deepened the warm flush already on her skin from the hot shower. "You don't have to say that."

"You expect me to lie?"

"Sawyer, I'm flat-chested and skinny."

"You're kidding me?" He stepped forward, tugged the towel from her hands and dropped it on the floor. He cupped her breasts, stroking his thumbs over the tips. His body saluted when her nipples pebbled and her breath hitched. "You're incredibly beautiful, and these are perfect."

Disbelief filled her eyes. How could she doubt her beauty? As much as he wanted to convince her, to push her back under the hot spray and lose himself inside her again, he forced himself to kiss the tip of her nose and step back. The passion marks on her body proved he'd ravaged her enough in the past few hours. "I have to swing by the paint store this afternoon. Want to tag along to look at nursery decorations?"

Interest flashed in her eyes, but then she glanced at the bed and bit her lip. "I should probably tackle the boxes."

He swallowed his disappointment. After last night he'd thought they didn't stand a chance, but then today she'd surprised him. He had a feeling he was moving too fast for her, but they'd made headway today. She claimed she didn't want love, but he wanted her love. Until her grief faded he'd have to be happy with whatever she would give him.

Lifting the tray from their late lunch, he told himself he shouldn't be greedy. He'd never spent half a day in bed with a woman before, but he hadn't been able to get enough of Lynn. Watching the surprise in her eyes and the aroused flush on her cheeks had kept him chained to the bed more securely than a pair of handcuffs. His blood heated and he shook his head. If he didn't get out of here now, then he'd never leave and no doubt she needed a break after the workout he'd given her.

Dipping his head he stole another kiss and then drew back and grinned. The flush tinting her cheeks couldn't be blamed solely on her steamy shower. "Trooper's been fed. Maggie and the other puppies are taken care of. I'll be gone a couple of hours."

Optimism added a spring to his steps as he descended the stairs. Lynn desired him and she *liked* him. He grinned at the adolescent thought. They would make this marriage work. If Brett's ghost couldn't keep them apart, then nothing would come between them.

The feeling of rightness as Lynn draped her afghan over the back of Sawyer's sofa and arranged her knick-knacks on his shelves stirred hope within her, but if there's one thing she'd learned it was that if a situation felt too good to be true then it wasn't going to last.

It was time to regroup, to reassess and rebuild the walls around her heart. The need for a reality check drove her back to Brett's journal.

One frustrating hour later she slammed the book closed. What did Brett mean when he wrote, "He had the upper hand as long as he held what Sawyer valued most?"

What did Sawyer value most? What could Brett possibly have that Sawyer wanted? The rings? The pocket watch? She didn't think so. Whatever it was, she needed to find it and return it. Why couldn't she figure it out?

She'd read the journal several times from front to back since Brett's death, but the only thing she'd succeeded in doing was make her head and her stomach hurt. Parts of the journal seemed to be written in half sentences with words out of place. Was it code? She couldn't be sure, but she had a feeling Brett had been anticipating something big in the months preceding his accident, and then whatever-it-was had happened. His tone had been quite smug in those last few entries. But what was he writing about?

The crunch of tires in the driveway jerked her out of the past. She jumped off the chaise, shoved Brett's journal back under the mattress and tried to shake off her funky mood, but it clung to her like skunk stench.

She met Maggie at the bottom of the stairs just as

Sawyer entered the front door. Lynn wished she could blame the quickening of her heart on her run down the steps instead of acknowledging where it really belonged—on the man in faded jeans and a snug T-shirt shouldering his way through the door.

This morning had been a revelation. Sawyer had made her feel cherished with everything he said and everything he did. He'd spent hours pampering her and pleasuring her. She'd never been so spoiled in all her life, and she'd certainly never thought of herself as a sexual being. Now she did. Brett had been wrong about her being frigid. What else had he been wrong about?

Part of her wanted to throw caution to the winds, to believe in the fairy-tale image Sawyer created and to let him work his mind-numbing magic so she could forget the past and not worry about the future. But she'd been burned by the last knight who'd swept her off her feet.

A teasing grin eased over Sawyer's face and sparkled in his eyes. "I like my women waiting for me at the door."

She wet her lips and took a steadying breath, but her insides quivered. When he looked at her as he did now with heat and hunger in his gaze she felt attractive, and when he touched her... Instead of freezing, she melted. His touch had soothed the hurts inflicted over the past few years, and after the last hour with Brett's journal, she desperately needed that balm again.

Sawyer set down the paint cans, hooked a hand behind her neck and kissed her slowly, thoroughly. Her stomach fluttered and her heart filled with hope...and then clenched. *Reality bites, remember?*

She wasn't falling in love with Sawyer, was she? No. Absolutely not. She didn't need to review Brett's condescending and cryptic notes to be reminded of what had happened last time she'd loved someone. Love had made her vulnerable. She'd become a powerless victim of Brett's whims. For her baby's sake she couldn't—*wouldn't*—let that happen again. But this isn't a love match, she reminded herself. This is a friendly cohabitation. She would come out of this marriage financially secure and hopefully still friends with the man who would share custody of her child.

See where this year takes us, Sawyer had said. He wasn't thinking beyond the term of their original agreement. She shouldn't, either.

He drew back and pulled a stack of booklets and brochures from beneath his arm. Lynn frowned at the familiar logo. ''What's that?''

''I stopped by the university admissions office and picked up a course catalog. The baby's not due until February. You can enroll in classes for the fall semester. The campus also offers programs that would allow you to study at your own pace from home after the baby is born.''

What he offered drew her, but at the same time the offer slipped over her shoulders like a straitjacket. She hungered for an education, for a way to stand on her own feet and support herself and her child with a decent job. But first she had her independence to establish. ''We've already been over this, Sawyer. I don't want to quit my job.''

His features tightened. ''When we were dating you couldn't wait to start at the university. Brett took that opportunity away from you. I want to give it back.''

''I have to settle Brett's estate and get ready for the baby.''

His jaw set in a determined line. ''Then perhaps I should make enrolling a job requirement.''

"You can't order me to take classes."

Muscles flexed in his jaw. "Dammit, Lynn, you have a knack for marketing. What you did with the flyer and with no formal training blows my mind. Consider how good you'd be if you had experts teaching you the tricks of the trade. You'd be phenomenal, even better than Brett, and he was a marketing genius."

His praise warmed her. "But I need my salary to pay off Brett's debts." She bit her tongue and prayed he'd miss her slip.

His eyes narrowed. "Brett's debts?"

"I meant the estate's debts."

Questions filled his eyes, but he didn't argue the point. "You can be a work-study student like our interns. Take a light course load and work part-time. I'll cover your tuition and book expenses. I only want what's best for you."

A chill slithered down her spine, chasing away the warmth of his praise. Brett had used that phrase with regularity—right before he'd told her something she didn't want to hear. "Don't ever say that to me."

He frowned at her sharp tone, and she grimaced. Reading the journal had sucked her right back into that negative place she'd been before Brett's death. She should have ignored it and finished unpacking the rest of her boxes. Maybe one of them contained the mysterious item Brett believed Sawyer valued so highly. "I'm sorry. I know you mean well, but I can't handle this many changes all at once."

His expression made it clear that he couldn't understand why she'd refuse the education she'd once passionately wanted, and she couldn't explain how trapped she'd felt during her marriage without tarnishing his mental picture of Brett.

Finally he shrugged and offered her a plastic shopping bag. "We're going out tonight. Wear this."

He'd hit another hot button, and her hackles rose again. What would she find in the bag? A skintight outfit like the ones crammed in her closet upstairs—the ones so tacky even the consignment shop wouldn't take them? Would Sawyer dress her up and parade her in front of his friends the way his brother had? God, she'd hated the way men looked at her in those skintight dresses. And the women... Dressing as if you might be interested in luring away someone's husband didn't exactly win friends and encourage lunch invitations.

She balled her fists by her side and refused to accept the bag. "I prefer to choose my own clothing."

His frown deepened. "Do you want to tell me what has you so edgy that you're ready to start a fight over a softball jersey?"

The knot in her stomach loosened. "A softball jersey?"

"The company team has a game tonight. I thought you might enjoy getting out and meeting some of the team members' spouses."

She winced and briefly closed her eyes. "I'm sorry."

"Lynn, what's going on?" His direct gaze and the stubborn set of his jaw said he wouldn't move until he had an answer.

Maggie, evidently sensing the tension between them, danced around their feet. Stalling for time, Lynn bent and scratched the dog. She couldn't tell Sawyer that reading his brother's journal had ripped the scab from all her insecurities and reminded her of what a fool she'd been in the past. She looked forward to the day when she could burn the book, but in the meantime, Sawyer needed an explanation.

"Brett used to choose all of my clothing."

She could almost see the Rolodex in his brain flipping through the suggestive clothing she'd worn with a different perspective. "And you don't want me doing the same."

"No."

"Because it reminds you that he's not here to do the job or because you don't want me dressing you like a sex kitten?"

Embarrassment scorched her cheeks at his harsh but accurate description, and she hated putting a chink in Sawyer's image of his brother. "It's time for me to make my own choices, including my clothing and my future."

"In most cases I'd agree. Lynn, you're a beautiful woman. You don't need to flaunt your assets to bring a man to his knees, and I sure as hell don't have any business choosing your clothes. But I want you to reconsider going back to school, for yourself, not for me." He tossed the university materials on the antique hall table and dropped the bag on the floor. "If you want to go to the game, I'm leaving in half an hour."

"What about Trooper?"

"He'll have to go with us." He turned on his heel and headed for the door, calling over his shoulder. "Come on, Maggie. Let's go for a walk."

The door closed. The course catalog drew Lynn like a magnet. She stroked her hand over the cover. What Sawyer offered sounded too good to be true. Did she dare trust him and take him up on his offer?

If she wanted to regain control, then getting the education Brett had denied her would be the first step. She would not let her past ruin her future.

Nine

The woman was a mass of contradictions. As soon as Sawyer thought he'd decoded the mystery of Lynn, she did something to confound him. Good thing he liked riddles.

What had happened during his two-hour absence? He'd left her soft, sexy and amenable, and then he'd returned to a porcupine. Everything he'd said had earned him a jab from her quills. But a porcupine only used its quills as a defensive measure. Did she regret making love? Or did she feel as if she'd betrayed his brother?

The more he learned about his brother's marriage, the less he realized he knew. It wasn't what Lynn said but what she didn't say that planted the questions in his mind and opened the acid floodgates in his stomach. The facts didn't add up.

He loaded the softball equipment and the water

cooler into the back of his Tahoe and mentally ticked off what he'd learned. Half the time Lynn seemed to be bracing herself. For what, he didn't know, but the tense set of her shoulders and the wariness in her eyes were hard to miss. And the way she responded like a flower turning toward the sun at even a hint of praise made him wonder if she'd not had much of it.

The yearning in her eyes when he'd offered her the university course catalog contradicted her stubborn refusal to enroll. Why refuse when he was willing to foot the bill, and why did she deny that Brett had made her drop out? What did she stand to gain by covering for his brother?

And then there were her clothes. Brett had dressed her in a way designed to make other men want her, and yet Lynn didn't have the confidence of a sex kitten. How could a woman with a body like hers not know her effect on men? It was obvious from her shyness and the self-contained way she moved that she didn't have a clue that rooms full of men suffered whiplash when she walked past. She didn't play to an audience.

And the biggest question nagging him: she didn't seem to be mourning his brother, and yet she'd been trying to have a baby with him. Did it have something to do with her I-want-a-marriage-but-not-love deal?

How could he woo his wife if he didn't understand her?

The back door opened, and Lynn, wearing shorts and the baseball jersey he'd brought her, stepped out on the porch. Her legs were long, lean, tanned and bare. Being tangled in them was as close to heaven as he'd ever been. Her all-American-girl freshness that was ten times more dangerous for his peace of mind than her knock-'em-dead clothing. Given the attraction between them, their basic belief in family and his love for her, he'd assumed that they could make this marriage work with a little effort. Now he suspected there might be several hidden obstacles in his path. "Ready?"

She jogged down the steps. Excitement and nervousness mingled in her eyes and pinked her cheeks. "Yes. I've never been to a company softball game."

"Brett didn't play." Come to think of it, Brett always managed to have a conflicting engagement whenever company events were scheduled. He didn't remember him bringing Lynn to any company functions, and Brett had rarely brought her to the office. Many of the folks she'd meet today would be strangers. Only a few of his employees' spouses had ventured to the funeral and even then, Lynn had kept to herself.

A line appeared between her brows. "No. He wasn't into sports. I'm not that athletically inclined, either."

An image of her sleekly muscled body flashed in his mind and heated his blood. "You swim like a fish."

Shadows filled her eyes. "I prefer it to exercise videos for keeping in shape."

Damn it. What wasn't she telling him? The strain in her voice told him there was more to the story, and he intended to learn all of Lynn's secrets—even if he didn't like the answers.

He opened her car door and assisted her inside. Once she'd settled herself in the seat, he leaned across to buckle her seat belt and kissed her. He reveled in the slickness of her tongue, the softness of her lips and the sexy little whimper she made when he cupped her breast. By the time he pried himself away they were both breathing hard, and his heart was trying to pound its way out of his chest.

He stroked a finger down her nose and over her damp

lips. "If this game wasn't part of the league championship, I'd drag you back upstairs." His words came out a little ragged.

He loved the way she blushed and the bashful way she ducked her head to hide her face. She'd been married for four years. How could she still blush over a kiss and a little flirtatious banter?

He nudged up her chin. "I packed snacks and drinks in the cooler. Eat before you get queasy."

"Sawyer—"

"I know. You can take care of yourself. Humor me. Let me get Trooper and we'll go." Sawyer shut her door, fetched the puppy's box and set his bundle on the floor behind the front seat. He settled in the driver's seat with a wry smile on his face. What was this? Practice for the baby and a car seat? Yeah, he liked the sound of that.

Before he knew it, the entrance to the city park loomed ahead. Unlike most of the women he'd dated, who filled every moment of silence with chatter, Lynn had remained mute during the ride. He pulled into a parking space behind the dugout and turned in his seat. "You want to tell me what upset you earlier?"

Lynn stared at her knotted fingers. "This morning was a little…intense."

His muscles clenched. "Regrets?"

She lifted her gaze to his and, sure enough, the wariness was back full force. "No. No regrets."

He released the breath he'd been holding, extracted his new family from the car and headed for the field.

Lynn nearly dropped Trooper's box when Sawyer put his fingers to his mouth and let out a shrill whistle.

Within seconds two dozen people surrounded them beside the bleachers. Sawyer set down the equipment bag and rested his hand on her shoulder. "Folks, this is Lynn. My wife."

Sawyer introduced her to the people she didn't know with a short descriptive phrase of who they were or what they did at Riggan CyberQuest. She'd met a few of the employees since starting her job, but names and positions swirled in her head. She'd never be able to keep them straight let alone remember all the spouses' names especially since *everyone* wore a red team jersey.

Sawyer hadn't bought her the jersey to make her stand out. He'd wanted her to fit in. Once more he'd included her in his circle as if she had every right to be there. The knowledge rattled the barriers she'd worked so hard to fortify.

Folks fussed over the sleeping puppy, and then a little girl around two or three years old toddled over and held up her hands. Sawyer scooped her up without hesitation and showed her the pup. After admiring the dog she cupped Sawyer's face with dirty hands and pressed a sloppy kiss on his cheek. He didn't object. Brett would have been horrified, and now that she thought back on it, Lynn wondered how she'd ever fooled herself into believing Brett would be a good father. Sawyer would be.

"Annie, you're getting Sawyer dirty." One of the women reached for the child.

Sawyer gave her up reluctantly, it seemed, and turned to Lynn. "Sandy and Karen can recommend obstetricians. Lynn and I are expecting."

He said it with a gentle smile in her direction that made Lynn's heart jolt in an irregular rhythm.

The umpire interrupted, telling them if they wanted to get this game in before the storm hit they'd better take the field. Off in the distance the sky had turned gray and threatening.

Sawyer escorted her to the bleachers and waited for her to settle. "Will you and Trooper be okay?"

"Of course."

He looked to the woman sitting on her right. "Sandy?"

"Got it covered."

Lynn stared after Sawyer as he jogged to first base. She tried not to notice how his white baseball pants hugged his firm backside and his thighs, but one thing led to another, and she recalled the taut firmness of his buttocks and thighs beneath her fingers and the unselfish way he'd pleasured her over and over until she'd begged him to stop. She marveled at the warm, tingly feeling in her stomach and the heat gathering beneath her skin. The fantasy pulled at her, but she tamped it down. This was not love. This was not a marriage made in heaven. There wasn't a happily-ever-after card in her deck.

She looked at the woman beside her. "Did he just ask you to baby-sit me?"

Grinning, Sandy bounced the toddler on her knee. "Pretty and smart. Guess Sawyer knows how to pick 'em."

Lynn laughed. She could hardly take offense.

The woman named Karen parked her stroller with a sleeping infant inside next to the bleachers and settled on Lynn's left. She gazed at the puppy in the box at Lynn's feet. "When's your baby due?"

"February, I think."

"You think? You haven't seen a doctor?"

"Not yet. We just found out." She refused to confess the shameful secret that she didn't know who had fathered her baby, and if these women knew about her marriage to Brett they were too kind to mention.

Sandy smiled. ''Sawyer will be a great dad.''

''I think so, too.'' Lynn felt like a teenager with a crush, sitting on the sidelines and cheering on the team captain. It was a new experience.

The women chatted about pregnancy and babies throughout the first three innings, pausing midsentence to cheer for the team and then resuming as if there'd been no interruptions. They made Lynn feel as welcome as an old friend. The instant acceptance was something she hadn't had in her adult life.

Children gathered around while she fed Trooper and then dispersed when she finished and returned the sleepy pup to his bed. Karen's baby awoke and lay in the stroller cooing and blowing bubbles.

Karen looked up and smiled. ''You'll have one of your own soon.''

The thought both excited and terrified Lynn. She touched her stomach. ''Yes, I can't wait.''

About halfway through the game another woman joined them, sitting down on the row above them. Sandy leaned forward. ''Lynn, this is Jane. Her husband's on third base. Jane, this is Lynn, Sawyer's wife.''

''Newlyweds, huh?'' Jane arched her dark brows. ''I can't blame Sawyer for rushing you to the altar. He's put his life on hold for that no-good brother of his. With Brett out of the picture Sawyer can make up for lost time.''

Lynn's blood ran cold. She couldn't move, couldn't think, couldn't reply.

''No need to get catty, Jane,'' Sandy said with a nervous glance toward Lynn.

''Who's catty? I'm stating facts. Brett was a liability.

He never did his part of a project on time. Jim always complained about him, and God knows how much overtime Sawyer had to put in to get Brett's share of the work done. Poor Sawyer, it's a wonder he had any life at all since he was always cleaning up after Brett.''

Lynn's nails bit into her palms. Her stomach churned. She hadn't known Brett shirked his work. In fact, he'd often claimed to be working late. *He'd probably been with his mistress.*

The game played on, but Lynn's enjoyment of the evening had vanished. She struggled to focus on the men and women on Sawyer's team and tested herself on their names—anything to keep from dwelling on Jane's words. Was she just another cleanup job Sawyer had assumed?

Despite the heat and oppressive humidity of the early-June evening, a cold sweat beaded on Lynn's upper lip. She felt sick. Sick at heart. Sick to her stomach. She turned to Sandy. ''Could you tell me where to find the rest rooms?''

Sandy rose, ''I'll show you. Karen will watch the puppy.''

By the time they made it to the small building housing the facilities, the churning in Lynn's stomach had subsided to a manageable discomfort. She splashed cold water on her face and sagged against the counter. Sandy hovered nearby, washing the worst of the dirt from her little girl's hands and face.

''Should I get Sawyer?''

''I'm already here.'' Sawyer loomed in the doorway.

Lynn's heart skipped a beat. He'd been covering for Brett for years. Was that what he was doing now by marrying her? Finishing a job Brett hadn't completed? Tears stung her eyes. She blinked them back.

She loved him.

"Don't you have any respect for the sign on the door?" She winced at her peevish tone. He'd done nothing to deserve her anger—nothing except make her fall in love with him.

"Not when you're in trouble."

"You're missing the game—a *championship* game."

He shrugged. "I was in the dugout when I saw you bolt up here. Are you sick? Do we need to go home?"

Sandy scooted past him. "We'll just leave you two alone. Take as long as you need. We have the puppy covered."

Lynn tried to return Sandy's sympathetic smile, but her lips quivered. "Thanks, Sandy. Tell the team Sawyer will be right back. I'm okay now, Sawyer. Go back to the game."

He stepped forward. "What happened?"

Her heart ached. She wanted to ball her fist and beat his chest. Why had he made her love him? She knew what would happen next. She turned on the faucet, splashed water on her face to hide her tears and then buried her face in a fistful of paper towels. "It's just the usual not-morning sickness."

He took the damp towels from her and gently wiped her face. From the black on the paper, she guessed her mascara was history. "Come and sit in the dugout with me."

She wanted to sob at the tenderness in his eyes. It looked real, but it couldn't be if she was an obligation. Brett had fooled her so many times with his false sincerity that she didn't dare believe. "I can't do that."

He smiled and pressed a kiss to her forehead. "Sure you can. Being the boss comes with perks."

Her time with Sawyer would end. All her relationships did. But until it did she could soak up every moment of every day storing up memories in her own mental photo album.

He laced his fingers through hers and led her back toward the field. They detoured by the bleachers to pick up Trooper and kept going. In the cool shade of the dugout he settled her on the bench and handed her a pack of crackers and a cold drink from the cooler. He sat beside her, wrapping his arm around her shoulders as if she had every right to be there, and he stayed until it was his turn to bat. Every moment was bittersweet.

Tears pricked her eyes as he stepped into the batter's box. How could she help but love him? Sawyer made her feel wanted and cherished in a way no one had since before her mother's death. He made her feel smart and beautiful and sexy. She leaned against the solid block walls and pressed the ice-cold soda can to her cheek.

Twenty minutes later thunder rumbled and then lightning flashed, closer now than before. The umpire called the game, and the players left the field. Sawyer and his teammates jogged back to the shelter to gather their gear.

He brushed a hand over her hair. "Stay put. I have to help put the equipment away and then we can go."

The rain began to fall. Sawyer left the dugout and waved the others toward their cars. They left him to pick up the bases alone. By the time he had everything locked in the storage building the rain poured. Lynn hugged herself as the temperature dropped in the deeply shaded concrete shelter.

Wet but smiling, Sawyer reentered the dugout and settled on the bench beside her, lacing his fingers through hers and stretching his long legs out in front of him. ‘‘Let’s give it a few minutes and see if the rain lets up.’’

For several minutes they sat in silence. She debated asking him if she was just another of Brett’s burdens, but decided she didn’t want to know the answer.

Sawyer lifted her hand onto his thigh. He traced a distracting pattern on the inside of her wrist with his thumb, drawing her out of her dark thoughts. She glanced at him, but his eyes were closed and his head rested against the back wall of the structure. He seemed unaware of the havoc his careless caress created inside her. And then his lids lifted, and she caught her breath at the smoldering desire in their depths. Maybe he wasn’t as unaware as she’d thought.

‘‘Ever made out in a dugout?’’

The wicked twinkle in his eyes set off a chain of tiny explosions in her bloodstream. She sucked in a surprised breath, and her stomach muscles fluttered. Sawyer may not love her, but he wanted her, and she was greedy enough to soak up his attention while she could. ‘‘No.’’

One corner of his mouth tipped up. ‘‘Want to?’’

She scanned what she could see of the now-deserted park, and a thrill raced over her skin. ‘‘We can’t. It’s a public place.’’

His brows waggled and his expression said, ‘‘So?’’

Her heart was breaking and he made her laugh. ‘‘You make me feel like a naughty teenager.’’

‘‘Is that a problem?’’ He slid closer and cupped her jaw.

‘‘I don’t know. I’ve never been one.’’ Her words trailed off when his lips brushed hers.

His brows rose. ‘‘The captain of the baseball team never put his moves on you?’’

"No. I wasn't very popular in high school," she admitted hesitantly. She didn't want to explain about the rumor that made her friends desert her in her junior year.

Disbelief filled his eyes and slowly turned to heat. He stroked the pulse at the base of her throat with his thumb, and then bent and sipped from her lips again. Drawing back a fraction of an inch, he met and held her gaze. "Let me show you how much fun we can have with our clothes on."

Her skin flushed and her body tingled. Fun? Sex had never been fun before. It had always been serious, intense and unsatisfactory business. Until Sawyer. She marveled at the way he could arouse her with nothing more than words. Why hadn't she experienced this before today? And would she ever again once this marriage ended? "Okay."

He kissed the corners of her mouth, her nose, her chin, making her desperate for his deep, drugging kisses. She chased his mouth with hers and finally caught his face in her hands and kissed him. She felt his smile against her lips, but he stubbornly waited until she licked the seam of his lips before opening his mouth over hers and letting her taste the slickness of his tongue. A duel ensued. Hot, long, wet kisses followed one after the other as she stockpiled memories.

Sawyer's fingertips skimmed her ankle, her calf, the sensitive seam behind her knee and then her thigh, sliding with agonizing slowness beneath the hem of her shorts. The tip of his finger eased beneath the elastic of her panties and her senses spun. She dug her nails into his back, wanting him to touch her, to recreate the magic he'd made this morning, but the fabric of her shorts impeded him. She'd never wanted to rip off her clothes before, but she did now and it surprised her.

His other hand skated over the slick fabric of her jersey, approaching her breast at a snail's pace. She fought impatience and dragged her nails up his back, urging him forward with a slight pressure. His wet shirt pressed against her chest and she gasped. "You're cold and soaked."

"And I'm going to get you hot and wet." He flashed a lethal grin and captured her breast in his hand, kneading her and plucking at her nipple.

Her breath hissed through her teeth as pleasure spiraled inside her. A shiver raced over her. Her breasts were overly sensitive from the attention they'd received that morning, but it was a good kind of tender. She pressed her hand over his, stilling him. He leaned back, his expression quizzical. "Tender."

He lowered his forehead to hers, pulled his fingers from beneath her shorts and captured her hands in his. "I'm a selfish SOB. I never considered that today might have been too much for you."

"No. I want you, Sawyer. I want this..." Her words dried up when she realized what she'd said. The words had come from her lips before. Brett insisted that she tell him she wanted him. But she hadn't meant it. Now she did. She wanted Sawyer, ached for him deep inside. She needed to feel the way only he could make her feel, and she wanted to look in his eyes, to watch him battle for the control and know that she had the power to push him over the edge.

She wanted to make love with him knowing she loved him.

"But?"

She'd never openly asked for what she wanted, she

realized, and that made her lack of physical pleasure before Sawyer at least partly her own fault. *Take control of your life. Take control of your passion.* "I want to touch your skin. I need to feel it pressed against mine."

She bit her lip at her boldness, but instead of offending him, passion flared in his eyes. His chest rose as he took a deep breath. "Let's go home before we get arrested for what I'm thinking."

He stood and pulled her to her feet. After covering the puppy's box with a towel, he put it in her hands and then slung the equipment bag over his shoulder and grabbed the cooler. His naughty wink sent her stomach plummeting. "Race you to the truck."

They were both drenched by the time they'd stowed their load and climbed into the front. Sawyer reached across the seat, snagged a hand behind her neck and kissed her until they were both panting. He cranked the engine and headed home. The sun, riding low on the western horizon, broke free from the clouds as they turned into the neighborhood. Sawyer pulled into the driveway, parked and silenced the engine.

Lynn's blood hummed in anticipation. She climbed from the vehicle before he could open her door, but he quickly caught up with her, took Trooper's box from her and set it on the patio table under the umbrella. He linked his fingers with hers and led her toward the pool.

She frowned. "Where are we going?"

"You wanted skin." His wet shirt clung to the muscular wall of his chest, revealing his beaded nipples. She didn't need to look down to know hers did the same. His white baseball pants were soaked and practically transparent. She could see that he wore nothing but his jock strap beneath.

"Yes, but..." Her words died when he pulled off his

shoes and dropped his keys inside of one. Her mouth dried when his shirt landed on top of them.

"Take off your shoes, Lynn." The husky rumble of his voice made her shiver.

Swallowing hard, she looked over her shoulders toward the neighboring house. "We're outside."

"Rick's not home and there's nothing but a hundred acres of woods on the other side of those magnolias. Nobody can see us." His baseball pants and socks landed on top of his discarded shirt.

The splendor of his naked, fully aroused body took her breath. Could she make this marriage work? Did she dare wish for more than the twelve months stipulated in their agreement? Hope flared inside her. She dug deep inside for the courage to do as he asked and toed off her shoes. He helped her peel the red jersey over her head, and then he outlined the lace edge of her bra. With a flick of his fingers the front clasp gave way. He dragged the straps over her shoulders, and her bra hit the ground. He unbuttoned her shorts and pushed those and her panties over her hips when she hesitated. She stepped free of the fabric and hugged herself.

In a swift move, Sawyer swept her into his arms and leaped into the pool with a whoop. The warm pool water, combined with the heat of Sawyer's skin, instantly banished the rain-damp chill. Her gasp of surprise turned into a sputter of laughter when she surfaced. The mischievous glint in his eyes made her smile. He wanted to play and so did she. With a swift kick, she ducked under the water and raced for the ladder at the end of the pool. He caught her three strokes later, encircling her ankle with his long fingers and tugging her back into his arms. She didn't fight hard.

Slick and wet, he slid against her. Their legs tangled.

Their bodies melded, hard chest to soft breast. His arousal prodded her belly and heated her blood. Knotting her fingers in his hair, she dunked him, twisted out of his arms and kicked free. He chased her toward the shallow end, but yanked her back into his arms before she could find her footing. Lynn's pulse accelerated, not out of fear or exertion but out of excitement.

Banding his arms around her waist, he backed her up against the cool wall of the pool. She couldn't touch the bottom, but he could. He stepped between her thighs. His thick, hard shaft pressed against her curls, and he flexed his hips. His hard shaft stroked her cleft and she gasped. Twining her arms around his neck, she depended solely on him to keep her afloat.

His hips pinned hers to the wall and his hands roamed freely, gently over her breasts, her buttocks, between her legs. Each hurried but tender touch expanded the need inside her. She mirrored him gesture for gesture. He stole a carnal kiss and caught her legs in his hands, winding them around his hips.

Surely he wouldn't be such a generous lover if he didn't feel something for her?

"Lynn." His voice sounded strained, like a man on the verge of losing control. For her. The knowledge glowed inside her. If she affected him half as strongly as he affected her, then maybe, maybe they had a future together.

She cradled his face in her hands. "Sawyer."

As if she'd whispered the magic word, he filled her with a slow, deep thrust. Her head tipped back against the smooth surround of the pool, and a moan escaped her lips. He devoured her neck, sucking hungrily as he withdrew and plunged again and again. With each thrust the pressure inside her intensified.

She caressed his slick skin, kneaded his taut muscles and his tiny beaded nipples. She fed off his ravenous mouth, and tension grew inside her. Hope grew. Love grew. She loved him. Loved him. Loved him. Waves of pleasure crashed over her, radiating out until even her toes tingled. And then Sawyer threw back his head, groaned and emptied himself deep inside her.

She feared this temporary marriage would lead to a permanent heartache.

Ten

The doorbell rang. Sawyer eased off the sofa, taking care not to wake Lynn from her Sunday-afternoon nap. He covered her with a knitted throw that she'd unearthed from her boxes.

She loved him. She hadn't said so yet, but surely love would explain the softness of her eyes and the tenderness in her touch. Of course, he hadn't confessed his love, either, but he would tonight over dinner.

He strode into the front hall and yanked open the door. Carter stood on the doorstep with a briefcase in his hand. The serious expression on his friend's face told Sawyer this wasn't a social call. Carter had found the thief. Adrenaline pumped through Sawyer's bloodstream. He motioned for Carter to come inside and then led the way to his study.

"Where's Lynn?" Carter asked.

"Taking a nap."

"Good." Carter closed the door, and the hair on the back of Sawyer's neck rose. He'd never known a more cool-headed person than Carter, but his friend was clearly nervous.

"Who?" The single word was all he could choke out through the tightness in his throat.

Carter faced him. "I triple-checked everything."

"And?" He moved behind his desk, grasping the edge and bracing himself.

"It's an inside job."

Sawyer swore. "Why would my staff want to steal from me? We have great morale and they're well paid. I know statistics support an inside job, but not by my team. We're like family. You must have made a mistake."

"I have the proof." Carter set his leather briefcase on the edge of the desk and flicked open the brass latches.

Pain over the betrayal filled Sawyer. Fast on its heels came rage. "I want the SOB's name. I want to know every time he accessed those files, every time he screwed me and with whom. I want to know who he sold the program to and how much they paid for it."

"It's all in my report." Carter hesitated until Sawyer wanted to shake the rest out of him. "Sawyer, I'm sorry. Brett was your mole."

Sawyer recoiled in shock. Denial screamed inside him. He went cold, but sweat popped out on his brow and upper lip. "You're wrong. Somebody laid a false trail and framed him."

"I found substantial deposits in his bank accounts coinciding with the dates you gave me—the most recent one and the one two years back."

He didn't want to know how Carter had gotten confidential bank information, but it didn't matter since *he was wrong.* "My brother would never steal from me."

Carter sighed. "You have to admit the competitive drive Brett had toward besting you with cars, homes, possessions, *Lynn,* could easily extend toward your business. He wanted what was yours."

"We had a healthy sibling rivalry. That's it." But what about the pocket knife, the ID bracelet and the rest of the jewelry? What about Lynn? He crossed his arms over his chest. "Why would Brett steal from the company that supported him?"

"Your brother owed money all over town. As far as I can tell, the bank had turned down his recent loan applications, and his credit cards were maxed out and past due. The only way he could get more money was to squeeze it out of you, but asking for it would have meant admitting he was in financial trouble, thereby losing his battle of one-upmanship."

The stack of bills he'd seen at Lynn's house substantiated Carter's statements, but he wouldn't believe Brett would betray him. "I know you didn't like Brett, but I never expected you would maliciously blacken his name."

Carter's face hardened. "Don't shoot the messenger, man. You've said yourself there's nothing I can't track. I wish I could pin this on somebody else. God knows I tried, but every lead circled back to Brett. As far as I can tell, he acted alone, selling trade secrets to one of your competitors."

Sawyer ground his teeth and turned his back on Carter. Why would Carter lie? But he *had* to be lying.

"Do you think it's easy for me to tell you this?"

He whirled around. "Then why did you if you're such a damned good friend?"

Carter exhaled heavily and held out his hands. ''I almost didn't, but I didn't want you worrying about the security of your company. With Brett out of the picture you can go ahead and launch your other projects without fear that those will be pirated, too.''

Sawyer shoved a hand through his hair. He'd done everything he could for Brett. He'd skimped and saved, budgeting to keep a roof over their heads and to put Brett through college. He'd given him a job and a share in his company. Brett would not betray him.

''Do you think Lynn knew what he was doing?'' Carter asked.

Sawyer sucked in a sharp breath at the unexpected attack. Every muscle tensed. ''No.''

''I know you've always had a soft spot for her, but you've got to face facts. Lynn benefited from Brett's excessive spending, and she sure as hell married you before the dirt settled on his coffin.''

''You're wrong.'' Anger tightened his chest. He fisted his hands and fought the urge to punch Carter's lights out. Why would his friend try to separate him from the two people he loved most? ''I don't know why you're determined to pin this on Brett or to drag Lynn into it, but you've screwed up your perfect investigation record. I'll write you a check for your services, and then I want you to get the hell out of my house.''

''You know I wouldn't lie to you about this.'' Carter withdrew a thick file from his briefcase and tossed it on the desk. ''Here's my data. When you're ready to pull your head out of the sand, you can read the facts for yourself.''

He wouldn't believe it. Couldn't believe it. ''Get out.''

A tense moment passed. ''When you're ready to talk, you know where to find me.''

''That won't happen.''

Carter turned on his heel and stormed out of the house.

The slamming of the front door jerked Lynn out of her horrified stupor. The raised voices had woken her, but the words had chilled her to the bone. *Brett was the thief.* How could she not have known?

The illogical ramblings in Brett's journal suddenly made sense. For whatever reason he'd fabricated in his irrational mind, Brett had felt justified in taking away what Sawyer valued most. He'd wanted what was due him, he'd written. Brett wasn't like Sawyer. He never took the hard way when an easier one presented itself.

Lynn's breakfast raced for her throat. She slapped a hand over her mouth and raced upstairs to her bathroom where she emptied her stomach. When her nausea finally subsided, she rose, washed her face and brushed her teeth. Sagging against the bathroom counter, she hugged herself.

What was she going to do?

Would Sawyer's love for Brett turn into hate? Would that hatred extend to Brett's baby and her? Since Brett was adopted, there wouldn't be any blood tie between Sawyer and Brett's child. She laid a protective hand below her navel and prayed that she carried Sawyer's child—not only for her child's sake, but for Sawyer's sake. He valued family above everything, and he needed this child to be his. He needed a family to love. She'd fallen in love with him. She didn't want to leave, but he had every right to order her out just as he had Carter.

If he kicked her out what would she do? The money

she'd expected from selling her share of the company back to Sawyer wasn't rightfully hers. She couldn't take it if Brett had stolen from Sawyer. She wouldn't take anything more from him. She laid a hand over her breaking heart and blinked back tears.

"Are you all right?" Sawyer's voice startled her. She jerked around to find him standing in the bathroom doorway.

"Yes. Are you?" She knew exactly how it felt to have your precious memories poisoned. Her heart ached for him.

"You heard." His assessing gaze swept over her.

"It was hard to ignore the yelling."

"I'm fine." Just as he had after the funeral, he tried to hide his pain from her, but it was there in the shadows of his eyes, the furrow in his brow and the rigid set of his shoulders.

She'd wanted to protect him from Brett's dark side and she'd failed because she'd underestimated Brett's treachery. Covering the distance between them, she wound her arms around his waist and laid her cheek over his heart. His stiff spine slowly relaxed and his arms encircled her. "I'm sorry."

"Carter thinks Brett was the thief." The pain and disbelief in his voice made her eyes sting. "Why would my best friend lie about something like that?"

The crack in her heart widened. This morning she'd believed she and Sawyer had a chance to make this marriage work. She loved him. He liked and desired her. Now, building on that foundation looked like an impossible dream. But she couldn't let Brett continue to rob Sawyer by costing him his best friend.

The only way to stop the destruction of the friendship was to share the damning journal that described her faults in excruciating detail. Once Sawyer read what a failure she'd been as a wife and as a woman, he wouldn't want anything to do with her. But did she have a choice? Carter had been with him longer, whereas she was only an obligation he'd assumed, another of Brett's messes to clean up. As much as it hurt her to do so, she had to sacrifice her love for his bond with Carter.

"He isn't lying. Brett did steal from you."

Sawyer abruptly released her and stepped back. "What are you saying?"

Why did the possibility of losing Sawyer hurt ten times more than Brett's cheating? Had she ever really loved Brett or had she been in love with the idea of love, enthralled with the picture of home and family he'd painted, back when he'd swept her off her feet? There was no comparison between the superficial emotion she'd felt for Brett and the deep, soul-pervading love she felt for Sawyer.

Lynn reached under the mattress and pulled out the cursed journal. "I found this after Brett died. In it he writes about 'holding on to what Sawyer values most' and 'getting his due.' There are dates—probably the same dates you gave Carter—where Brett talks about his ship coming in."

When Sawyer wrapped his fingers around the journal's leather binding, Lynn silently said goodbye to her hopes and dreams for a happy marriage. "Brett has already taken enough from you, Sawyer. Don't let him drive a wedge between you and Carter."

His eyes turned hard. His lips thinned into a flat line. "You knew what he was doing and you covered for him."

Her blood ran cold. Suddenly dizzy, she staggered to

the door frame for support. She didn't know what to say. There were no magic words to change the past.

"You covered for him because you still love him," he accused.

No! But she couldn't tell him she didn't love Brett or that on that fatal night she'd almost hated his brother for what he'd done to her and hated herself for what she'd surrendered to her marriage. His disgust made her stomach threaten another revolt.

She swallowed her nausea. "I didn't tell you because I didn't want to ruin your memories of your brother. Brett's gone. His crimes ended with his death. Your company is secure."

He cursed, paced to the window and spun to face her. The agony in his eyes made her gasp. "You betrayed me. Just like my brother."

She pressed a hand to her chest. "Sawyer, I would never do anything to hurt you. I love you."

He recoiled as if she'd struck him. "Do you think I'll believe that now? You're trying to cover your ass. You love my brother enough to lie for him even after he's gone." He shoved a hand through his hair, and that curl that she loved fell onto his forehead. She yearned to pull him close and brush it back, but he wouldn't welcome her touch now.

"Did you have sex with me after the funeral to cover your bases? Maybe you hoped to trap me into protecting you. And, fool that I am, I sapped up the story that this might be my child."

The knife in her heart gouged deeper. "You know that's not how it happened, and it *might be* your baby."

"I don't know what to believe anymore. I thought I took advantage of you, but it looks like I had that backward."

"No, I—"

"The people I trusted most in the world have cheated and lied to me."

"I didn't know until—"

"You knew Brett was screwing me and you didn't tell me. That's all that matters." He turned his back on her. The tension in his shoulders revealed his battle for control. "I'm going to take Maggie for a walk."

"But—"

"I need to get out of here, to figure out where our marriage stands." He turned and headed out the door.

Tell him.

"Sawyer, wait." He didn't pause. His steps clattered down the stairs. He whistled for Maggie, and then the front door slammed on all her dreams.

Sinking onto the chaise, she didn't try to stop her tears. Should she stay and fight for her marriage or scurry to her aunt's in Florida like the timid little mouse she'd pretended to be for the past four years?

Get out of Sawyer's house and his life before he kicks you out, the coward in her urged, but the fighter in her reminded her that her daddy had always said nothing worth having comes easy. Fearing rejection, she'd let Brett run roughshod over her dreams, and she'd paid for her cowardice. She'd lost herself, her soul in her first marriage. If she loved Sawyer she had to tell him the truth—*the whole truth*—and risk rejection.

And then Trooper whimpered. Lynn dried her eyes and tended to the puppy, because no matter how bleak things looked, life went on. And she wasn't a quitter.

How in the hell had he been so blind?

Sawyer dropped Brett's journal onto his desk and buried his face in his hands. How could he not have seen the malice in his brother? He and Brett had always been competitive, but the actions Brett had boasted about in his journal—using many of the secret code words the two of them had developed as kids—went far beyond a healthy rivalry. His brother had been willing to lie, cheat and steal to best him, and it hadn't mattered who got hurt in the process.

Lynn. Sawyer clenched his teeth until his jaw ached. Brett hadn't loved Lynn or cherished her the way she deserved. He'd used her, possessed her, dressed her and flaunted her like a trophy. All those puzzling clues finally made sense. No, she didn't know how to receive pleasure. No, she'd not been given any praise. Yes, she'd been bracing herself for an attack. Had Brett limited himself to verbal abuse?

Nausea roiled in his stomach and anger fired his blood.

What in the hell had she endured as a pawn in Brett's game of tormenting Sawyer with what he couldn't have? And why hadn't she ever spoken of the misery she must have faced behind closed doors? Had she really fallen for his brother's sappy apologies? Brett bragged that she did, but Lynn was too smart for that.

How could she love such a monster? But she must love him or she wouldn't keep covering for him. Sawyer rubbed the ache in his chest. *She still loved his brother.*

Brett's derogatory comments sickened him. His brother didn't think Lynn was smart enough, sexy enough or pretty enough. Sawyer had never met a smarter, sexier woman, and Lynn was beautiful inside and out. God, he loved her laugh, her thirst for knowledge, the way she'd turned his house into a home in just a few short days.

Brett had called her frigid. Had his brother been crazy? Lynn was the most responsive lover Sawyer had ever had, but how could she melt all over him if she still loved Brett? His mind tumbled with the contradictions of what he'd once thought versus what he now knew. What was fact and what wasn't?

He blamed himself. He'd found Lynn first, and if he'd spoken directly to her before leaving town four and a half years ago instead of trusting Brett to deliver a letter—a letter he suspected Lynn never received—she wouldn't have suffered the indignity of having the man she loved tell her she wasn't woman enough for him without plastic surgery. He silently applauded Lynn's bravery in refusing to go under the knife, but what had her refusals cost her? The journal had revealed a vindictive side to his brother that he'd never seen.

Bile burned the back of his throat. He'd once threatened that if Brett ever hurt Lynn he'd make his brother pay. Brett had hurt her all right, over and over, and then he'd done whatever it took to hold on to what Sawyer valued most. *Lynn.*

He'd been too blind to see his brother's machinations.

Sawyer rose and stared out the window. He loved Lynn with all his heart, but he'd let her down. First by failing to protect her from Brett and then by forcing her into a marriage she didn't want when she still loved and grieved for Brett.

Though it hurt more than anything he'd ever faced before, he knew what he had to do. He had to set Lynn free.

He headed for the door on leaden legs and found her in the kitchen preparing dinner. Her eyes were puffy and rimmed with red. Her face looked drawn and her bottom lip swollen as if she'd been chewing on it. Her hands trembled as she set the dishes on the table. After one hit-and-run glance, she wouldn't look at him.

He shoved his fists in his pockets and fought the urge to hold her. "I'm sorry."

She stopped in her tracks and lifted her gaze to his, but she remained mute, clenching the back of a chair until her knuckles turned white.

"I'll see my attorney first thing in the morning to arrange for a divorce."

She inhaled sharply, paled and after a moment nodded. "I understand."

"I'll get a loan to buy your share of the company."

"I won't let you do that, Sawyer. Brett has already stolen from you. You shouldn't have to keep paying for his mistakes. I'll sign my share over to you."

He wouldn't let her do that, but he didn't want to argue now. "I'll pay you a monthly allowance, and I'll pay child support, but I'll relinquish my paternal rights."

He tried to ignore the tears pooling in Lynn's eyes and then streaking down her face, but each one burned him like acid. He cleared his throat, but the knot remained stubbornly in place. "I don't know where I went wrong with Brett or what I could have done to make him hate me. I don't understand what he thought he'd gain by destroying the company that paid his salary. Hell, another incident like this and Riggan CyberQuest would have folded. He would have been out of a job. Maybe that's what he wanted—to destroy my dream. I don't know where I went wrong," he repeated.

"You didn't," she whispered.

He snorted his disbelief. "If I messed Brett up this badly in only a decade imagine what I could do to your child in an entire lifetime. It scares the hell out of me."

"Sawyer, you can't blame yourself for Brett's greed."

"I won't inflict myself on you or the baby you're carrying."

She crossed the kitchen and laid a hand on his forearm. "I can understand why you'd shun Brett's child, but if this is your son or daughter, then he or she deserves the right to know you. Don't let Brett's actions make you believe you'd be anything but a wonderful father."

Stunned, he gaped at her. "You'd be willing to risk me turning your kid into a felon?"

"That wouldn't happen. Brett didn't hate you, Sawyer. He worshipped you, and he wanted to be just like you. Only, Brett was lazy. He wasn't willing to work for what he wanted. He took shortcuts. That's not your fault."

Even now she covered for Brett. Jealousy and pain threatened to choke him. He shook off her touch, because it only made him want to hold her more, and scrubbed a hand across his face. "He abused you verbally. Did he ever hit you?"

"No. Never. If he had I would have left."

"He treated you like crap, Lynn. Why cover for him?"

"Because family is the most important thing in the world, and I didn't want your memories of Brett to be tainted. When memories are all you have left, those memories should keep you warm at night instead of haunting your dreams." She paced to the back door, turned and faced him.

"You knew my father was a cop and that he was killed in the line of duty. What you probably didn't know was that the ensuing investigation turned up a suspicion that he'd been a dirty cop. He was never cleared but never found guilty, either. That didn't stop the papers from crucifying him or my aunt and me since he was already gone. All of my memories of my daddy have been poisoned. When I think of him now, instead of remembering a man who loved my mother so much that he almost died when she did, I remember those last days. The detectives took our house apart. They went through every closet, every drawer. *They went through our trash.*''

Tears rolled freely down her cheeks, and the knot in his throat thickened until he could barely breathe. ''I remember being told the man I thought was a hero was really a crook who took advantage of the people who counted on him to take care of them. I didn't want you to suffer like I did.''

She looked so shattered and vulnerable. He stopped fighting his need to hold her and pulled her into his arms. He kissed her hair and rubbed his cheek against the soft strands. Her honeysuckle scent filled his senses. ''I'm sorry.''

She shrugged and pulled free.

''How could you still love Brett after the way he treated you?''

She looked away and then her shoulders sagged. When she met his gaze again, his stomach clenched at the pain in her eyes. ''I didn't.''

''What?'' He grabbed her shoulders. ''Tell me the truth this time. All of it. Don't try to pretty it up to save my feelings.''

She hesitated so long he thought she'd refuse. ''Brett and I had been having trouble for a long time. I'd already talked to a lawyer about filing for a divorce, but Brett convinced me that his bad attitude was caused by job stress. He promised he'd get better, and he dangled the chance to start the family I'd always wanted in front of me. I wanted a baby so badly that I was stupid enough to give in.

"That night, after we made love I found out he'd been cheating on me *with Nina.*"

Sawyer swore. He should have suspected something when Brett hired an assistant whose bust measurement was higher than her IQ.

Lynn took a deep breath. "We had a huge fight. I lost my temper and screamed at him to get out of the house. I told him I would file the divorce papers the next day. An hour later he was dead. So while you're hating Brett, you might as well save a little of that hatred for me. If I hadn't lost my temper, he might still be alive."

"Lynn, he was driving ninety miles an hour in a thirty-five-mile-an-hour zone. You can't blame yourself for that. We're damned lucky he didn't take somebody out with him. And from the garbage he's written in his journal, I think you were entitled to lose your temper."

"You still blame yourself for the accident that claimed your parents."

"Yes."

"What's it going to take to get through to you? The other guy was *drunk*. It was dark. *He* ran the light, *he* didn't have on his headlights. You're not being logical."

Some of the weight lifted from his shoulders. "Yeah. I guess you're right."

Lynn headed for the stairs. She had to get out of here before she lost control. A sob burned deep in her chest, and in two more seconds she'd be bawling like a baby.

"Why do you care?" Sawyer's question halted her on the bottom step.

What did she have to lose? She'd already lost it all. Without turning she said, "Because I love you, and I believe you're the one who said, 'Love doesn't quit when the going gets tough.'"

Quick steps crossed the tile floor and then his hand trapped hers on the newel post before she could retreat to her room. "Dammit, Lynn, don't you dare tell me you love me and then walk out on me."

She stiffened her spine and bit down on her quivering bottom lip.

He stroked her spine and she shivered. "Look at me. Please."

Slowly she turned. Her position on the bottom stair put them at eye level. What she saw in his deep-blue eyes made her tremble.

"You read Brett's journal. You must know that I love you."

She couldn't breathe; her head spun. "There's nothing in that journal about love. It's filled with hate and what a horrible wife I was."

One corner of his mouth lifted in a sad smile. Tenderness softened his eyes. "You're a perfect wife. Fun and sexy and so damned hot in bed that you make me lose it like an adolescent every time."

A spark ignited in her womb and radiated outward. She tried to snuff it out, because hope brought disappointment.

Sawyer's fingers drew tiny circles on the back of her hand, and the fine hair on her body rose. "Brett wrote that as long as he held what I valued most he held the upper hand. What I valued most was *you,* Lynn."

Her knees buckled. Sawyer caught her in his arms

and carried her into the den. He sat down on the sofa with her in his lap and stroked a finger down her cheek. ''When we met five years ago I knew you were special. What we had was amazing. But you were young, barely nineteen, and I had to spend so much time on the road trying to grow the business that I thought we should wait. When I was called out of town unexpectedly with an offer for a contract that could get the company off the ground and keep it running for years to come, I knew I finally had something to offer you, and I didn't want to wait any longer.

''We had a date that night, but I couldn't reach you to cancel it. I asked Brett to meet you, instead, to explain and to give you a letter that I'd written for you.''

Lynn gulped air. She wanted to believe what he said so badly, but she was afraid to get her hopes up. ''Brett didn't give me a letter.''

''I suspected as much from what he wrote in his journal. He must have opened it and read it to know how I felt about you. In the letter I wrote that I loved you, and that I wanted to spend the rest of my life with you. I wanted to see you as soon as I returned home, but I knew I'd be gone for months. I asked you to wait for me.''

A sob rose in her throat. Lynn slapped a hand over her mouth to contain it.

''And then I returned home to find you married to my brother.'' The honesty and pain in his eyes convinced her he told the truth.

She leaned her cheek against his and stroked his bristly jaw. ''I thought you'd dumped me. Brett said… He said you told him it was fun while it lasted, but that it was time for a taste of California girls. I turned to him on the rebound. I let him charm me out of my heartache. I feel like such a fool.''

''We were both fooled.''

''I'm sorry.''

''Me, too. Now, would you tell me the truth about enrolling at the university?''

She sighed. ''Most people see education as a chance to spread their wings, to gain freedom. For me it became the opposite. When I quit my job, Brett made me account for every penny of his money I spent and for every second of my time outside of the house. He sabotaged my study time. My grades suffered. Eventually he made me doubt whether or not I was smart enough to be a student.''

Sawyer swore. ''And you quit.''

''Yes.''

He laced his fingers with hers and kissed her fingertips. ''Lynn, I railroaded you into this marriage. If you want out, if you want your freedom, I'll let you go, and I'll pay for your education.''

Her heart swelled. ''I don't want out. I want to stay with you and raise a family with you. But, Sawyer, you need to understand that I'll love this baby even if Brett is the father.''

He palmed her belly, and her blood pooled beneath his hand. ''I will, too, because it's a part of you. I love you, Lynn.''

''And I love you.''

Epilogue

Sawyer pushed open the front door. Trooper barked and danced around his feet. ''Yeah, buddy, your momma's home and so is your new baby brother. Calm down. You're deafening me.''

Behind him Lynn laughed. She did a lot of that these days, and it grabbed him every time. Grinning, he dropped the house keys back into his pocket. His breath caught and his heart swelled the way it did every time he looked at his wife and his son. *His* son. Lynn took a step forward, but he stopped her. ''I didn't do this the first time I brought you home as my wife.''

He swept her and her precious bundle into his arms. She squealed. ''I'm too heavy.''

''You're perfect.'' He carried her over the threshold and set her down in the front hall.

She gasped. ''Oh, my gosh. What did you do? Buy

out the florist? There must be a hundred red roses in here."

"Happy Valentine's Day. And there are six dozen roses—one dozen for each Valentine's Day we should have spent together."

She smiled that tender, you-shouldn't-have smile that turned him to mush on a regular basis. "You have to stop showering me with gifts. You don't owe me for the past."

He bent and kissed her gently, tamping down the hunger that gnawed at him, and then brushed his lips over the pale-blue cap on JC's head. "Spoiling you is my job."

Gravel crunched as Carter's car pulled into the driveway. Trooper streaked outside to greet the newcomer and then barked even louder as Maggie and Rick strolled through the magnolias. Rick pitched a tennis ball, and both dogs streaked after it.

"So, did you make it through the delivery without hurling or passing out?" Rick asked as he and Carter climbed the front steps. The dogs charged past them and settled on the rug in front of the blazing fireplace.

Sawyer grimaced. "Near miss."

Lynn's chuckle skipped down his spine like a caress. "You did wonderfully once you settled down. It was the hour after my water broke that had me worried. Thanks for driving us to the hospital, Rick. Sawyer was a little nervous until we arrived and the doctors convinced him everything was proceeding as planned."

Rick laughed. "A little nervous? He was a basket-case."

Carter stepped forward. "So, let's see the little guy."

Lynn angled the baby toward them, and Sawyer tugged the knitted cap from his son's head revealing a shock of black hair. A moment of stunned silence greeted them.

Carter frowned, looked at JC, at Sawyer and then back again. ''He looks just like you.''

Discovering that he was the baby's father had been a wonderful surprise. They'd never explained about their forbidden encounter in the foyer. Lynn had been afraid his friends would think less of her for sleeping with him on the day of Brett's funeral. And if that was the way she wanted it, then his lips were sealed, despite his desire to shout the news of his son's birth from the rooftop.

Her smile and the happiness in her eyes put a lump in Sawyer's throat. He couldn't speak.

''Yes, he does,'' Lynn said quietly. ''He looks exactly like his daddy. He has those Riggan blue eyes and that straight little nose, and I'm guessing that's going to be the same stubborn chin. I have Sawyer to thank for helping me through a very difficult time and for giving me this very special gift.''

Carter was the first to recover, but he didn't voice the questions in his eyes. ''So what does JC stand for, anyway?''

Lynn laid his son in the bassinet beside the sofa and slowly unwound the extra blankets the cold weather required. ''Joshua Carter. Joshua after my father and Carter after the man who agreed to be his godfather.''

Carter swallowed hard and then turned his head. Sawyer saw him blink a few times before he faced them again. ''So does this make me an honorary uncle?''

Sawyer clapped him on the shoulder. ''You bet it does. Both you and Rick. Lynn and I figured we'll give you all the practice you need at baby-sitting and diaper changing so you'll know how to handle your own kids when the time comes.''

Rick jumped back with an appalled expression on his face. ''Whoa. Don't be shoving me down the aisle. I like being a bachelor.''

Lynn just smiled. ''You'll change your tune as soon as you get that promotion. Just wait and see. You'll want someone to share that big, rambling house of yours.''

''I have Maggie, and the mutt is the only female I need living under my roof.''

Sawyer pulled Lynn into his arms and looked deep into her eyes. He kissed her brow, her cheek and her nose. ''Trust me, guys, once love grabs ahold of your heart, you'll change your tune. And you won't ever regret it.''

Rick groaned. ''Here they go again. Come on, Carter, let's see what we can rustle up for dinner. If I know Sawyer, he probably planned to serve the new mommy Frosted Flakes.''

Carter and Rick headed for the kitchen.

Sawyer wasted no time in capturing Lynn's sweet lips. She kissed him back, and suddenly the six weeks until they could make love yawned like six years. He brushed a strand of golden hair from her cheek, eased her coat off her shoulders and tossed it over the back of the new rocking chair. ''Thank you for being the best thing that ever happened to me.''

She gave him a watery smile. ''Thank you for showing me what love is all about.''

''My pleasure.'' He reached into his pocket, withdrew his mother's silver-heart locket and then flicked it open to show her the pictures inside.

Her teary smile put a lump in his throat. ''My two

men. You and JC. I love you, Sawyer, more than I ever thought possible.''

''And I love you.'' He looped the chain over her neck. ''We'll have to keep trying for that daughter, but for now, why don't you hold on to this?''

''It's only fitting because you are in my heart.''

''And you, Lynn Riggan, are in mine.''

* * * * *

Watch for Emilie Rose's next Silhouette Desire,
on sale February 2005.
BREATHLESS PASSION
promises to sweep you off your feet!

COMING NEXT MONTH

#1627 ENTANGLED—Eileen Wilks

Dynasties: The Ashtons

Years ago, Cole Ashton and Dixie McCord's passionate affair had ended when Cole's struggling business had taken priority over Dixie. Now, she was back in his life and Cole hoped for a second chance. But even if he could win Dixie once more, would Cole be able to make the right choice this time?

#1628 HER PASSIONATE PLAN B—Dixie Browning

Divas Who Dish

Spunky nurse Daisy Hunter never thought she'd find the man of her dreams while on the job! But when a patient's relative, athlete Kell McGee, arrived in town, she suddenly had to make a difficult decision—stick to her old agenda for finding a man or switch to passionate Plan B!

#1629 THE FIERCE AND TENDER SHEIKH—Alexandra Sellers

Sons of the Desert

Sheikh Sharif found long-lost Princess Shakira fifteen years after she'd escaped her family's assassination. As the beautiful princess helped heal her homeland, Sharif passionately worked on mending Shakira's spirit. Though years as a refugee had left her hardened, could the fierce and tender sheikh provide the heat needed to melt Shakira's cool facade and expose her heart?

#1630 BETWEEN MIDNIGHT AND MORNING—Cindy Gerard

When veterinarian Alison Samuels moved into middle-of-nowhere Montana, she hardly expected to start a fiery affair, especially with hunky young rancher John Tyler. To J.T., this tantalizing older woman was a stimulating challenge and Alison was more than game. But J.T. hid a dark past and Alison wasn't one for surprises....

#1631 IN FORBIDDEN TERRITORY—Shawna Delacorte

Playboy Tyler Farrel was totally taken when he laid eyes on the breathtakingly beautiful Angie Coleman. She was all grown up! Despite their mutual attraction, Ty wouldn't risk seducing his best friend's kid sister until Angie, sick of being overprotected, decided to step into forbidden territory.

#1632 BUSINESS AFFAIRS—Shirley Rogers

When Jenn Cardon placed the highest bid at a bachelor auction, she had no idea she'd just landed a romantic getaway with sexy blue-eyed CEO Alex Dunnigan—her boss! Thanks to cozy quarters, sexual tension turned into unbridled passion. Alex wasn't into commitment but Jenn had a secret that could keep him around...forever.

SDCNM1204